"You talk about s

He tipped his arro⟨...⟩d at the yellow sofa tucked behind him. One damn look loaded with suggestion.

"Shut up and listen to me." She barely resisted the urge to stomp her foot.

"I am. It's fun to watch your cheeks go pink." He clapped a hand on his chest. "And by the way, my mother always told me it's rude to tell people to shut up." A sardonic smile played along his lips.

"Rude? Talking about sex in a business meeting is rude." She scooped up a brass paperweight in the shape of a bear that had belonged to her father. "I'm not in line to join the Alaskan female dating population ready to fawn over you."

"I didn't ask you to, and there's no need to threaten me with your version of brass knuckles. You're safe with me." Humor left his face and his expression became all business. "But since you're as bemused by this data as I am, come with me to speak to your mother."

"Of course. Let's do that. We'll have this sorted out in no time."

The sooner the better.

She wanted Broderick Steele out of her office and not a simple touch away.

* * *

The Baby Claim is part of the Alaskan Oil Barons series, the eight-book saga from *USA TODAY* bestselling author Catherine Mann.

Dear Reader,

Happily-ever-after comes in so many forms at many stages. My parents were high school sweethearts, and I was lucky to see them celebrate their fiftieth anniversary. Mom and Dad celebrated that milestone by driving around town in a vintage MG that my father had restored for the event. They visited local places where they had dated as teenagers. My mother was bedridden with lupus at the time and my father carried her to the car. There was no doubting their love for each other.

My mother passed away not too long after that, a day before their anniversary. We all grieved, but we also wanted Dad to find joy again—as Mom would have wanted.

And he did. My father met a lovely widow. They dated, married and are like giggly newlyweds. As my dad said, "Who would have thought my heart could go pitter-patter again?"

As we blended two families, the idea for this series came to me. What a joy it is to see it in print, a living testament to love's enduring power!

Happy reading,

Catherine Mann

www.CatherineMann.com

CATHERINE MANN

—

THE BABY CLAIM

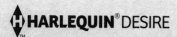

HARLEQUIN® DESIRE

Recycling programs
for this product may
not exist in your area.

ISBN-13: 978-1-335-97131-9

The Baby Claim

Copyright © 2018 by Catherine Mann

Printed in U.S.A.

USA TODAY bestselling author **Catherine Mann** has won numerous awards for her novels, including both a prestigious RITA® Award and an *RT Book Reviews* Reviewers' Choice Award. After years of moving around the country bringing up four children, Catherine has settled in her home state of South Carolina, where she's active in animal rescue. For more information, visit her website, catherinemann.com.

Visit her Author Profile page at Harlequin.com, or catherinemann.com, for more titles.

To Dad and Betty, and the joy of a
second happily-ever-after.

One

"Do you live to infuriate me, or is it a pleasant pastime for when you're not wining and dining the single females of Alaska?"

Glenna Mikkelson-Powers splayed her hands on her day planner to avoid launching herself from behind her mahogany desk to confront Broderick Steele.

Being so close to the man had never been a wise idea.

The sensual draw was too strong for any woman to resist for long and stay sane. His long wool duster over his suit was pure Hugo Boss. But the cowboy hat and leather boots had a hint of wear that only increased his appeal. His dark hair, which attested to his quarter Inuit heritage, showed the first signs of premature gray. His charisma and strength were as vast as the Alaska tundra he and she both called home.

In a state this large, there should have been enough space for both of them. Theoretically, they should never have to cross paths. But their feuding families' constant battle over dominance of the oil industry kept Glenna and Broderick in each other's social circles.

Too often for her peace of mind.

Even so, he'd never shown up at her office before.

She pressed her hands harder against her day planner and fixed him with her best icy stare. "I have an assistant. Zeke—the grandfatherly looking gentleman— can announce you. Or you can knock. At least attempt some semblance of a normal greeting."

Not that anything about Broderick was in any way calm or normal.

"First of all—" he tossed his snow-dusted hat on her desk "—I do not live to infuriate anyone. Your assistant wasn't out there."

Glenna glanced through the open door and found his statement to be true. She repressed her inclination to roll her eyes anyway. Surely Broderick could have waited for Zeke to return instead of barging in here.

"Second..." He peeled off his leather gloves one at a time, revealing callused hands. A man of brawn, he also happened to have an extraordinary chief finance officer aptitude that had served his family's business well. "...I am far too busy to have the sort of sex life you've attributed to me."

That dried up any words she might have spoken, and made her stomach flip more than it should have.

"Third, Glenna, I have no idea why you're acting like the injured party when I'm the one who had a bombshell dropped on my desk today." He leaned closer, the musky scent of his cologne teasing her senses like breathing in smoky warmth on a cold day. "Although once we sort this out, let's come back to the obsession you have with my sex life."

Light caught the mischief in his eyes, bringing out whiskey tones in the dark depths. His full lips pulled upward in a haughty smile.

"You're being highly unprofessional." She narrowed her own eyes, angry at her reaction to him as she drank in his familiar arrogance.

Their gazes held and the air crackled. She remembered the feeling all too well from their Romeo-and-Juliet fling in college.

Doomed from the start.

And yet…those memories had never faded.

One weekend long ago. A passionate couple of days in her attic apartment. Fireplace blazing. Snow piling on the skylight.

Steam filling the shared shower stall.

Still, those two days were nothing compared to the love she'd felt for her late husband during her six-year marriage. The deep emotional connection, the respect they'd felt for one another. The work they'd invested in overcoming hardships.

And the grief they'd shared over their inability to conceive a child.

Her job was everything to her now. Glenna refused to put it at risk, especially for Broderick.

He was her rival. He wanted his family's business to dominate the oil industry and she simply could not allow that. She was the CFO of Mikkelson Oil, and she'd make sure *her* family's business came out on top.

His mesmerizing eyes and broody disposition would not distract her.

She eased back in her chair. "This is the last time I will ask you. What are you doing in my office?"

"Like you don't know." He dropped a large envelope on top of her day planner. "What would you call this?"

"Mail," she said, giving herself time to figure out his game.

So much had been upended in the company since her father had died of a heart attack two years ago. So much loss. First her father, then her husband. She'd been left reeling. But if she allowed grief to consume her, Mikkelson Oil would lose out…to Broderick.

"Do you care to elaborate?" she asked.

He shrugged, his starched white shirt rustling against his broad shoulders.

"Printouts, technically, with some kind of bogus report on a stock share buyout. It makes no damn sense, but my people have traced it back to your office."

She reached into a drawer, pulled out a manila envelope and placed it next to his file.

"Really?" She tapped the envelope. "Because I could ask you about a similar buyout. In reverse."

His forehead furrowed before he dropped into one

of the two leather club chairs in front of her desk. "Our companies are exchanging shares? That doesn't make sense."

She jabbed a manicured finger in his direction. "Your father is up to something and I don't appreciate this push-back since my dad died. It's sexist to assume we're weaker without a man at the helm."

Her shoulders went back defensively as she sat taller and straighter. She would not allow Broderick Steele or his father to intimidate her.

"You talk about sex a lot." He tipped his arrogant head to the side and glanced at the yellow sofa tucked behind him. One damn look loaded with suggestion.

"Shut up and listen to me." She barely resisted the urge to stamp her foot.

"I am. It's fun to watch your cheeks go pink." He clapped a hand to his chest. "And by the way, my mother always told me it's rude to tell people to shut up." A sardonic smile played along his lips.

"Rude? Talking about sex in a business meeting is rude." She scooped up a brass paperweight in the shape of a bear that had belonged to her father. Shifting it from hand to hand was an oddly comforting ritual. Or perhaps not so odd. When she was a small girl, her father had told her the statue gave people power, attributing his success to the brass bear. After the last two years of loss, Glenna needed every ounce of luck and power she could get. "I'm not in line to join the Alaskan female dating population ready to fawn over you."

"I didn't ask you to, and there's no need to threaten

me with your version of brass knuckles. You're safe with me." Humor left his face and his expression became all business. "But since you're as bemused by this data as I am, come with me to speak to your mother."

"Of course. Let's do that. We'll have this sorted out in no time."

The sooner the better.

She wanted Broderick Steele out of her office and not a simple touch away.

Broderick was pushing his luck with Glenna, but this woman got to him in a way no one else ever had.

When they were in college, he'd told himself it was the warring-families, forbidden-fruit thing that had drawn them to each other. Except, he still craved her.

Usually he kept those feelings in check by staying as far away from this particular blonde bombshell as possible.

But today he'd received disturbing paperwork about stocks changing hands.

"Are you ready to speak to your mother about this now? We need to know who on your board, or on mine, is messing with our companies."

She looked up, her blue eyes as crystal clear as the Alaska sky after a storm. "Yes, absolutely, the sooner the better. She's here today. I met with her earlier this morning." Glenna nodded, rose and stepped to the front of her desk.

Holy hell. He damn near swallowed his tongue.

Her pencil skirt hugged her curves and set his imagination on fire. The suit jacket plunged, and even though a white blouse covered almost all her skin, that *V*... He forced his eyes away out of respect.

And to preserve his sanity.

"After you," he said.

He worked to keep himself in check, to stay steady even though proximity to her sent him reeling. He followed her past a sitting area in her office with that yellow sofa and two chairs clustered around a fireplace.

She glanced over her shoulder, blond hair swishing in a golden curtain. "Mother's office is two floors up. We'll settle this. Not to worry."

Without another word, she charged through the door, boot heels muted against the plush carpet. The wall of windows along one side of the corridor provided an awe-inspiring view of the mountains. It might be spring everywhere else in America. But here in Alaska, snow still capped the peaks.

Sunshine streamed through the windows and over Glenna. To keep his eyes off her swaying hips and the killer leather boots, he checked out the art on the other wall. Yet again he was struck by the differences between the Mikkelson corporate offices and his family's building on the other side of Anchorage's business district. The Steele headquarters had a more modern look, sleek and tall in a way that reminded him of his home state, like an ice sculpture filled with coal and grit and gold.

The Mikkelson offices harkened back to old-school Alaska, with a rugged elegance denoted by pelt rugs and wooden furniture heavy enough to remind people nothing fragile lasted in this land. To make it here, you had to be born of sturdy stock.

The file crinkled in his grip as they walked, reminding him why he was here. What did his father know? Broderick hadn't been able to find him this morning, and he'd tried hard. Damn hard.

Lately, his dad had been distracted and inaccessible. Unusually so, and at the worst possible time. Bids were going up for the major pipeline from Alaska to the Dakotas. This wasn't just about money or energy independence. It was also about keeping projects ecologically friendly, making sure the land they loved and called home was protected.

They were a family of engineers and ecologists, working like hell to present a balanced plan.

Broderick knew his reputation for being a cold bastard, but he didn't see the point in getting emotionally invested in anything—or anyone—outside of work.

Something had gone haywire in him when his sister died. He understood it intellectually, but that didn't make it easier to get past. Maybe if he hadn't lost his mother at the same time, she might have helped him find his way out of the maze where he sabotaged relationship after relationship. Now his dating life consisted of women who had no interest in anything more than being casual.

Glenna often stated—emphatically—that she was all about her job. He understood. He was married to his work, too.

That's why this ridiculous rumor of a merger had to be squelched.

"You don't act like most number crunchers."

He cocked his head to one side. "Practical, you mean?"

"I guess. You're just so…outrageous. Illogical. Unpredictable." She picked up her pace.

"And you are very much a buttoned-up numbers gal." Heat fired inside him as he thought of a time he'd *un*buttoned her, very thoroughly.

She seemed to read his mind. "Keep your eyes forward, cowboy."

"Do you think I brought a hidden camera to steal secret formulas from your office?"

He met her eyes full on and found those blue depths too alluring. Something about them made words slip out before he could stop them. "I would very much like to know your secret desires."

Her breathing deepened, her chest rising and falling quickly. She licked her lips. "I prefer we keep things all business. Do you think you can respect my wishes for at least the next half hour? If not, we'll be doing this meeting via videoconference."

He nodded, backing up a step, knowing he was playing with fire. Still, she was right about him being unpredictable. Despite the complications, he found himself plotting to press for more from her. Later, of course. Timing was everything.

"Of course I'll respect your wishes."

"I wish I could trust that," she said softly, before walking to the elevator and pushing the button.

Her words stung. Did she think so little of him? He joined her at the elevator, watching her, musing.

She felt for a hairpin, tucking it inside a sweep of hair that pushed the golden length over one shoulder. Her pale pink nail polish was barely perceptible. Classy. Understated. Like her. "I can't help but be concerned about you getting an insider's peek at our business and financials."

The elevator dinged, the doors slid open and she stepped inside.

He joined her in the circular enclosure, which provided a panoramic view of the harbor with a few boats still floating between chunks of ice. "Maybe you should worry about your files. There are all sorts of cloning devices for computers and—"

"I'll have the security guards strip-search you on the way out."

Just as he'd decided her word choice was accidental, she glanced back over her shoulder, blue eyes glimmering with mischief.

Heat spread and he moved to her side, ducking his head toward hers. "Will you personally supervise the search? Lucky for me I wore my favorite comic-character boxer shorts."

She arched one delicate blond eyebrow. She'd always had a way of putting a person in his place quietly, succinctly. "You flatter yourself."

"I dream, oh lady, I dream."

She tipped her head, her eyebrows pulling together. "I have to ask. Do you treat all business professionals this way?"

"Only the business professionals I've already had

an affair with. Actually, strike that." He held up a hand. "Only you. Everyone else at work, it's all business."

"A poor choice during one weekend in college is not the same as an affair." Her hands on her hips accentuated her curves in that killer power suit.

He ached to peel it off her.

Broderick clapped a hand to his chest. "You wound me. That weekend is my benchmark for all other relationships. Every woman falls short after you."

Had he really said that out loud? It had almost felt like he'd meant it.

He was saved from pondering that uncomfortable thought when the elevator bell dinged. They'd reached their destination.

Glenna surprised him by pressing the button to keep the doors closed. "Your board of directors may buy your bull, but I'm not fooled by your smooth talk."

She was right. Whatever he was doing with her, it had no place in the office.

But they were in the elevator. Alone.

He was not one to let an opportunity pass by.

He stepped closer, inhaling the scent of her. Almonds… Unexpected. Sensual. "What if I'm serious?"

Her eyes widened before she touched his elbow. "Then I am so very sorry you were hurt." Her throat moved with a swallow. Then her elegant nose scrunched and she pointed a slim finger at him. "But I'm not buying that line about all women falling short. Now stop playing me and let's speak to my mother."

Glenna let the elevator open, then charged ahead of

him around a corner to an empty receptionist's desk. "I'm not sure where Sage is—"

Glenna's young cousin Sage Hammond rounded the corner just then, smoothing her simple turtleneck sweater dress as she took her place at her chair. "I've been away from my desk. I was meeting with your assistant in the tech department. I'm sorry to have left things unattended. Your mother was busy with a call when I left." She tapped the phone console, strands of her whispy blond hair falling across her shoulders. "But the light's off now so she must be finished, if you wish to go inside."

Broderick nodded. "Thank you, Miss Hammond."

Glenna muttered, "Eyes off my cousin," as she reached for the door handle of the next office.

Jealous? Interesting. "I don't pluck wings off butterflies."

Glenna's sky-blue eyes shifted with something he couldn't name, just briefly, then she turned away and walked into her mother's office.

The interior held more of that Mikkelson charm. Antiques and splashes of light green filled the room, as if to bring life inside. Two walls of windows let sunlight stream into the corner office, and more rays poured through a skylight. Outside, the streets teemed with people, cars and even an ambling moose.

But the office itself was empty.

"Mom? I'm here with Broderick Steele. There's been a misunderstanding, a rumor we need to clear up." Glenna looked around. "I know she's here. There's her leather portfolio bag and her coat, even her cashmere scarf. She must be getting coffee."

Or in the powder room? Glenna's gaze flicked to the private bathroom.

Muffled sounds came from within, like a shower maybe, soft and indistinctive. Steam seeped from under the door as if the water had been running a long time. A moan filtered through. From an enjoyable shower? Or was that a sound of pain? He wasn't sure.

Broderick backed into the sitting area, away from the line of sight of the bathroom. "I'll step out so you can check on her. If you need any help, just say the word."

"Thanks, I appreciate that. Mom?" Concern laced Glenna's voice. "Mom, are you okay?"

There was no answer.

Glenna looked at Broderick. "I hate to just burst in, but if she's ill… If it's an emergency…"

"Your call. Do you want me to leave?" Maybe health issues might explain the strange business behavior.

"How about you stay back, but nearby in case I need to send you for Sage." Glenna tapped lightly on the door. "Mother, it's me. Are you all right?"

He studied the top of his boots, keeping his eyes averted.

"Mother, I'm worried. I don't want to embarrass you, but I need to know you're okay. I'm coming in."

When the doorknob rattled, Broderick glanced up and saw Glenna shaking her head. His concern ratcheted a notch higher.

"It's locked." She knocked harder on the door.

"Mom, you're scaring me. Open up. Please." She reached into her pocket. "I'm going to use my master key to come in." She opened the door—and squeaked.

She clapped a hand over her mouth, launching Broderick into motion. He rushed forward and rested a palm on her back, ready to help with whatever crisis might be unfolding.

Glenna pressed a steadying hand on the bathroom door frame. "Mom?"

Broderick stopped short. Blinked. Blinked again. And holy crap, he still couldn't believe his eyes.

Glenna might have been surprised, but Broderick was stunned numb. He even braced his booted feet because his world had done a somersault.

Jeannie Mikkelson stood wrapped in a towel in the steam-filled, white-tiled bathroom, and she wasn't alone.

An all-too-familiar figure edged in front of her—pushing Glenna's mother safely behind his broad chest.

Confused, Broderick couldn't stop himself from asking the obvious. "Dad?"

Two

Pacing in her mother's reception area, Glenna struggled to push through the fog of…confusion? Shock? She didn't know how to wrap her brain around what she'd seen, much less put a label on it.

Her mother was having an affair with their corporate enemy.

Okay, so, technically, Glenna had done the same in college, but she and Broderick hadn't held positions in the family businesses then. Even now they weren't the owners and acting CEOs of both companies. They weren't the parents who had perpetuated the feud with dinner table discussions of suspicions and rumors.

Back in college, Glenna had felt so guilty, like such a turncoat because of her attraction to Broderick. She'd felt that way just fifteen minutes ago in her office.

Now, she glanced across the waiting area at...the son of her mother's lover, boyfriend, whatever.

This was so surreal.

And Broderick was still infuriatingly hot. But things were more complicated than they'd been before, which had been mighty damn complicated.

He rested one lean hip against a wingback chair, his booted foot tapping restlessly. Her cousin looked back and forth between them. Sage obviously sensed something was wrong, but she kept her lips pressed closed. She wouldn't ask.

And she wouldn't gossip. Very likely that had been a quality high on Jeannie Mikkelson's list when she'd chosen her assistant.

Did Sage already know about the affair? And perhaps about whatever was going on with their stocks? If some hint of the relationship between the two oil moguls had leaked, that could explain the odd fluctuations in stock holdings as investors grew unsure, some selling off their interests while others scooped up more, based on their own hypotheses.

So many questions.

Starting with...how long did it take to throw on some clothes? Glenna winced at the thought.

The door to her mother's office finally swung open, the Alaskan yellow cedar panel revealing her mom, with Jack Steele standing tall right behind her, a gleam in his green eyes. Protective. Territorial. An unrelenting look Glenna had seen before in his business dealings. But this was different. So different.

She shifted her gaze to her mom.

Her mother's damp hair was pulled back in a clip, but otherwise there was no sign of what had happened. Jeannie Mikkelson was as poised and strong as ever. She'd run the corporation alongside her husband for years, and then taken the helm alone after his first major heart attack debilitated him.

She'd kept the business running at full speed through his entire health crisis and even held it together after that final fatal heart attack. The whole family had been rocked. But Jeannie? Glenna had seen her cry only once.

Her mother excelled at keeping her emotions under wraps.

So it was no surprise she remained unreadable now. This wasn't about her mother having a relationship with someone other than Glenna's father.

It was about her mom having a relationship with *this* man.

Jack Steele looked like an older version of his eldest son, with dark hair more liberally streaked with gray. He'd kept in shape, but age had thickened him. He was a character, similar to all three of his sons. He was executive and cowboy. And Alaskan.

One of the many headlines from his magazine profiles scrolled through her mind. *The CEO Wore Mukluks.*

Jeannie nodded toward her assistant. "Sage, could you hold all my calls and redirect any visitors?"

"Of course, Aunt Jeannie." Sage already had her notebook tablet in hand and was tapping with delicate efficiency.

"This may take a while."

"I'll reschedule your eleven o'clock and send Chuck to take him out to lunch."

Chuck, aka Charles Mikkelson III, was Jeannie's son, Glenna's brother and second in command of the company. Heir apparent to take over when Jeannie retired.

If she ever retired. Jeannie was still vibrant and going strong, only in her sixties.

"That's the perfect plan. Thank you, dear." Jeannie waved Glenna and Broderick into the office and Jack closed the door behind them, clicking the lock to ensure there would be no interruptions.

Glenna swayed and Broderick palmed her waist. She couldn't help but be grateful for the momentary steadying, even as his hand seared her.

Jack raised one eyebrow before saying, "Let's all have a seat."

Glenna self-consciously stepped away from Broderick, the tingle of his touch lingering.

The Steele patriarch pulled one of the green club chairs closer to the other, then touched Jeannie's arm lightly as she took her seat. He eyed the sofa, making it clear that Broderick and Glenna were to park themselves on it like two kids waiting to be put in their place.

Broderick still wasn't speaking, although he settled beside her on the apple-green sofa. Glenna couldn't get a read on him, but then her brain was jumbled again just by the simple brush of his knee against hers.

What the hell was it with the Steele men?

Her mother and Jack were now holding hands like teenagers. It was sweet—sort of—but still such a jarring sight. "Mom, I know this is your personal business and I don't want to pry, but you have to understand how confusing this is, given our families' histories."

"I realize this is more than a little awkward, Glenna, and we'd hoped to talk to everyone as a family soon."

Broderick tapped the file against his leg. "Talk to us about…which part? The relationship between the two of you, or is there something else you want to share? Something, say, business related."

Jack's thumb caressed Jeannie's wrist. "We want you both to know that this has come as a surprise to us, as well. Nothing happened while either of us was still married. We were very happy in our marriages."

Her mom leaned forward, reaching out to Glenna. "I loved your father, you know that. I still do."

Jack cleared his throat. "Son, you understand how…difficult… How…your mother's death…"

Looking over with a sympathetic smile, Jeannie squeezed his hand before continuing, "Jack and I have spent a lot of time together these past months dealing with different EPA issues and concerns with the economy."

"But our companies are in competition," Glenna pointed out, still not understanding the situation.

"Our companies were eating each other alive. We

would have been at risk from a takeover by Johnson Oil United. Their CEO, Ward Benally, has been making acquisitions and filings on their behalf that are concerning. We decided, out of a love for what we've built and for our home state, that we needed to talk."

Talk? Glenna couldn't help but note, "Clearly you've been doing more than talking."

After the words fell out, she winced at her own lack of diplomacy.

Her mother, however, laughed with a light snort. "Clearly. We were as surprised as you are." She tipped her head to the side. "Well, maybe not literally as surprised as the two of you were when you opened that bathroom door."

Jeannie's mouth twitched at the corners, then laughter rolled out of her. Jack's deep chuckles joined hers and they exchanged an unmistakably intimate look as they sagged back into the chairs, hands still linked.

For some reason, that moment made Glenna far more uncomfortable than seeing them in towels earlier. This was about more than sex. This truly was a relationship, a connection, something she didn't have in her life anymore, now that her husband was dead.

She might not have been married as long as her mother, but Glenna understood the pain of widowhood. And her deepest regret beyond losing him? She didn't even have a child of theirs to love.

Glenna pinched two fingers to the bridge of her nose, pressing against the corners of her eyes, where tears welled. So much loss. So much change. Too much for her to process.

Broderick inched forward and slapped the file down on the coffee table. "If we're all done with laughing, let me get this straight. The data and rumors that point to a merger of our two companies are not rumors. You're genuinely planning to dismantle both corporations, and you expect us all to join forces without input or discussion."

"No," Jack stated.

"Of course we don't," Jeannie echoed. "We're all adults and we have always intended to treat you as such. Things just happened so quickly between us we haven't had a chance to bring you up to speed."

"But," Jack interrupted, "we intend to. And soon. Very soon, son."

Broderick frowned. "Please say you don't intend to put us all in a room together, Dad."

"Not for the initial discussion," his father answered. "We are smarter than that."

Good thing. Being this close to Broderick, even for such a short time, was interfering with Glenna's ability to focus. And it seemed she would need to keep her wits about her now, more than she'd realized even a half hour ago. "Mom, what exactly do you have in mind?"

"We want to arrange family meetings separately first," she explained, her blue eyes worried but resolute. "We'll need to allow everyone time to process what we have to say."

"But then…" Jack held up a finger in a lecturing style that made Glenna wince. He wasn't her father.

And he wasn't her boss. Yet. "We fully expect every-one to accept our decisions."

Broderick gave a hefty exhalation as he sat back for the first time. "Dad, I think you're expecting a lot awfully fast." He turned to Glenna. "I don't know about your family, but my brothers and sisters? They're going to blow a gasket."

Glenna was completely in sync with Broderick on that point at least. Because expecting her siblings to end a decades-long family feud after a simple con-versation, expecting them to accept what appeared to be a blending of the businesses, too?

Blow a gasket?

Understatement of the year.

Broderick had eaten in restaurants around the globe, with food cooked by the finest chefs, and he'd enjoyed every meal.

But none of them outstripped the cuisine here at Kit's Kodiak Café in the little town outside Anchorage. The diner, a rustic barn type structure, was perched along the bay's edge. The paned windows presented a clear view of a dock stretching out into the harbor, an occasional whale's back cresting through floating chunks of ice. Inside, long planked tables accommo-dated large, noisy groups—like his family.

Menus crackled in front of the others, but he knew what he wanted, so his menu stayed folded. He flipped his coffee mug upright to signify java would be welcome. The waitress took their orders with quick efficiency and no pandering, another reason they all enjoyed coming here. Their family was well known in this café, but they appreciated not receiving special treatment.

He and his siblings had been coming to Kit's since they were children. Their father brought them most Saturday mornings and sometimes before school so their mother could sleep in. He would bundle them up. Half the time, their gloves didn't match, but they always had on a hat and boots as they piled into the family Suburban.

Broderick hadn't realized then how his billionaire father was trying to keep them grounded in grass roots values by taking them to "regular Joe" sorts of places, the kind that played country music and oldies over the radio. The air smelled of home cooking and a wood fire. Back then, he'd thought the stuffed bear was cool, the music loud enough and the food almost as good as his mom's.

And he still did.

As kids, the Steele pack had ordered off the Three Polar Bears menu. He'd taught his younger siblings to read their first words from that menu, even though they always ordered the same thing: reindeer sausage, eggs and massive stacks of pancakes served with wild berry syrup.

These days, he opted for the salmon eggs Benedict.

Their dad always said their mom had the hardest job of all, dealing with the Steele hellions, and the least he could do was give her a surprise break. He'd rolled out that speech at the start of every breakfast, and reminded them to listen to their mom and their teachers. If there were no bad reports, then they could all go fishing with him. Looking back, Broderick realized his father had done that so they wouldn't rat each other out and would solve squabbles among themselves.

It had worked.

He and his siblings had a tight bond. A good thing, sure, but both a blessing and a curse when they'd lost one of their siblings in that plane crash along with their mom…

Even when the table was full, it felt like there was an empty place without their sister Breanna there. Sometimes they even accidentally asked for six seats.

Today, though, their uncle sat with the five remaining Steele children, pulling up an additional chair as he joined them.

Uncle Conrad, their father's brother, hadn't been a part of building the Steele oil business. He was fifteen years younger than Jack, and had been brought into the company after finishing grad school with an engineering degree. He'd been a part of the North Dakota expansion. The Steeles had started in Alaska and moved toward the Dakotas, and the Mikkelsons had grown in the reverse direction, each trying to push out the other.

Uncle Conrad reached for the coffee carafe as he scooted his chair closer to the table. "Where's my brother? He's been in hiding since those rumors started flying yesterday morning. Damn rude of him to wait so long to meet with us. Marshall, Broderick? Somebody?"

CATHERINE MANN31

"I only just got here. I was out with the seaplane, surveying," Marshall pointed out. The family rancher, he oversaw their lands, as well as doing frequent fly-overs of the pipelines.

Conrad cupped his coffee mug in his hands. "You'd think he would have returned calls from his own brother."

The youngest Steele sibling, Aiden, reached for the pitcher of syrup. "You would think so. It sucks being discounted because you're the last in line." He smiled, but it didn't reach his eyes. A thick lock of hair fell over his forehead. "Right, Uncle Rad?"

"Don't call me that, you brat. You're as bad as your brother here." Conrad gestured to Broderick. "You both carry that sardonic act a little far. We're your family. Tell us, Broderick, is it true that you and Glenna Mikkelson-Powers found your dad with…"

Conrad shuddered and took a bracing swig of coffee, then refilled his mug, emptying the carafe. He held up the silver jug and smiled at the waitress as she swept it from his hand on her way to another customer.

"I couldn't begin to say what you're all envisioning. And it was even tougher to see…" Broderick leaned toward his youngest sister.

"Tough to comprehend," Delaney responded, spooning wild berries onto her oatmeal.

Naomi, the wild child, older than Delaney and the boldest, most outspoken sibling of the pack, leaned her arms on the table. "Was he really going at it with Jeannie Mikkelson?"

"In the shower?"

"In her office?"

The questions from both brothers tumbled on top of each other.

Broderick forked up a bite of salmon and eggs. "Sounds like you don't need me to tell you anything."

Naomi slathered preserves on her toast. "What the hell is up with Dad?"

Conrad lifted his coffee mug. "Oh, I think we all know what's up."

Delaney snapped her napkin at him before draping it in her lap again. "Don't be crude."

"He's older, as am I—" Conrad waggled his eyebrows "—but not dead."

"Eww." Delaney pushed her oatmeal away, her dark eyes widening and her nose scrunching. "Too much information."

A cluster of tourists walked by the table, cruise ship name tags on lanyards around their necks. The Steeles went silent until they passed.

Naomi tapped a pack of sweetener against her finger before opening it into her coffee. "Do you think that's all it is? An affair with a Mikkelson, the forbidden fruit?" She slanted a glance at Broderick. "I mean, you had that—"

Broderick leveled narrowed eyes at his sister and mentally cursed himself for a drunken admission in a quest for advice.

"Okay, okay." She opened another packet of sugar into her coffee. "Damn, everyone's testy around here."

"Well…" Delaney admitted softly, "I did get Dad

on the phone, and while he wouldn't give me details, he admitted they're in love."

A series of hissed breaths and heavy exhalations sounded, along with silverware clanking.

"Broderick," their uncle interjected, "what do you think? You actually saw them together."

"I would say Dad's serious about her," he answered without hesitation.

"You don't think this has been going on for a long time? A very long time?" Naomi's dark brown eyebrows, already plucked to high arches, went even higher.

"Could be, but they say their feelings caught them by surprise. I choose to believe them."

"How serious do you think this is? Like…marriage? What's going to happen to the business?" Marshall forked a hand through his loose brown curls, his face full of questions.

Delaney stirred the berries through her oatmeal before spooning up a bite. "Were you able to get details about their plans? Do they want to make changes to the company's safety standards?"

Broderick shook his head. "We didn't get that deep into the discussion. Dad said he wanted to speak to all of us at the same time Jeannie Mikkelson speaks to her children, but separately."

Aiden pulled three more pancakes from the platter in the center of the table. "I'm still stuck on the fact our families hated each other for years."

"Maybe just the fathers?" Delaney asked quietly.

Broderick shook his head. He knew differently, firsthand. He and Glenna both did. "Jeannie Mikkelson was as much a part of that business as her husband. She's different from Mom."

At the mention of their mother, his siblings went silent in a new way, leaving a heavier atmosphere around the table. None of them had really come to peace with losing her or their sister Breanna in such a violent and unexpected way. A plane crash into a mountain... There hadn't been much left in the wreckage after the flames. Their father had been allowed to view the bodies, but he'd kept his children away.

Broderick could see the memories ripple across each face at the table.

Naomi finished chewing her toast and took a swallow of her coffee. "Maybe this group meeting with Dad will be a golden opportunity to get him to see that...hell, this is a mess for the business. The board will go haywire over this. The stockholders will react violently to the uncertainty."

Broderick scrubbed his hand along his jaw. "You're going to tell them to break up for the sake of profit? That's not going to float, not with our dad."

His youngest brother's eyes went wide with a hint of fear, giving Broderick only a moment's notice before a familiar voice rumbled over his shoulder. "What's not going to float with me?"

His father.

Jack Steele had arrived.

Three

Broderick carefully set aside his coffee mug as he crafted an answer for his father that wouldn't send the old man—and the table full of edgy people—spinning.

His family had a way of letting their tempers fly. Especially since the peacemakers had died...his mother, his sister. These days, Delaney often tried to rein in family squabbles, but she was only one soft voice against a tide of pushy personalities.

Just as he was about to opt for a Hail Mary distraction instead of a logical plea, he was saved from answering when Conrad stood and pulled up another chair.

"Have a seat, Jack. You're the man of the hour. We've all been on pins and needles, waiting to hear from you about your, uh, *news*." Conrad clapped his brother on the back.

"Thank you for meeting me here on such short notice." Jack waved to the waitress as he took his seat. "The usual order for me, please," he called, requesting sourdough waffles, as he had for decades. The only difference lately? These days he topped the waffles with fruit rather than syrup.

They'd gathered at this table more times than Broderick could count, until it had become a de facto family dinner table. One his father loomed large over when sitting at the head.

Being Jack's oldest son hadn't been easy. Broderick's father's boot prints in the snow were large to fill and he cast a long shadow in the business world.

But damn it all, Broderick wouldn't stand idly by and watch the Steele business be placed at risk. He knew Glenna felt the same about her family's legacy.

Strange to be on the same side with her.

Broderick watched his father with analytical eyes. He wasn't going to weigh in recklessly. He needed to wait for the right opportunity and choose his words wisely. The stakes were too high for misplaced speech. The fate of his company—and his place within the family business—depended on rationality, not impulse.

Conrad took his seat again. "Thank you for putting your clothes on for us. Poor Broderick here still looks like he needs a bracing drink."

Jack scowled, his lips so tight his mustache all but hid them. "You can zip your mouth, brother."

Conrad smiled unabashedly. "Do we really want to talk about zippers right now?"

Leaning back in his chair, Jack crossed his arms over his chest. "My sense of humor on this has run out. You're being disrespectful to Jeannie and I won't stand for that."

"Fair enough," Conrad conceded. "You have to understand we're all more than a little stunned by what's transpired."

To hell with waiting. Broderick saw the opening to take control of this conversation, not only for his family's sake but also for Glenna's. "We grew up believing our families to be enemies. I can't count how many times I've heard you curse both of them—Jeannie and Charles Mikkelson."

"Things change," Jack said simply, pouring a mug of coffee. The statement was casual, as normal as the black coffee he had drunk every day for as long as Broderick could remember. "I don't have to explain myself to any of you, but I will say that Jeannie and I love each other. Very much. We intend to be married—"

"Married?" Aiden interrupted, his voice cracking on the word.

Everyone else stared in stunned silence, then looked at Broderick as if he'd kept a secret from them. Shaking his head, he pressed his fingers to his temples against the headache forming. He'd had no sleep, instead wondering how serious his father's relationship with Jeannie really was, if it might wane with time. A litany of questions had kept him awake. Not to mention being tormented by visions of Glenna in that tight skirt every time he closed his eyes. Seeing her again had brought back memories, vivid ones.

"Yes," Jack confirmed, in a no-nonsense tone, the kind he'd used on his children when they were younger, "married. Sooner rather than later, especially now that our secret is out. Jeannie and I discussed it at length last night, which was why we didn't answer any of your phone calls."

Broderick focused on a crucial word in his father's answer. "Sooner?"

"Yes, now that you know, why wait for the perfect time to break the news? Jeannie and I *had* planned to tell our children in a more…prepared, controlled manner this weekend. But yesterday afternoon's events forced our hand. Jeannie is speaking with her children now." He glanced at Broderick. "As I'm sure you already know from talking to Glenna."

The mere mention of the Mikkelson CFO drew a few raised eyebrows at the table. His siblings looked at him with sidelong glances, understanding that their father had tipped the balance of power in the conversation. Shifting slightly in his chair, Broderick pushed the image of Glenna and her sunset-blond hair out of his mind. Far away.

Broderick had no intention of letting his father distract them from the topic at hand. After all, the old man had taught that diversionary tactic to each of his kids.

Leaning forward with elbows pressed on the wood table, Broderick levied his own power. "Let's stay on target, Dad. You're here to fill us in on your engagement plans to a woman we thought you didn't like. Do I have that right?"

"More than engagement plans. As I said, we are getting married." His tone was as stern and certain as an Alaskan winter.

"A long engagement?" Broderick said it hopefully.

The extra time would give their relationship a chance to cool. Perhaps even allow Jack to see the madness of this whole situation. To really evaluate what this meant for their companies.

Jack's eyes warmed, wistful and sentimental. Something Broderick hadn't seen in his father's expression since before the plane crash.

"*Short* engagement."

"How short?" Naomi asked. She was more of a daddy's girl than she liked to let on.

Jack waited until the waitress set his waffles in front of him and walked away before he continued. "Jeannie and I are getting married on my birthday. Surefire way I'll never forget my anniversary." A smile cracked his wind-weathered face and a slight chuckle escaped his mustached lips. Jack had clearly amused himself.

The hair stood up on the back of Broderick's neck. A guttural, visceral reaction to the realization of what his father was saying. "Your birthday is—"

"In two weeks." Jack's chin dipped with a quick affirmation.

"Oh God," Naomi whispered, but every member of the Steele clan felt the words echo deep in the pit of their stomachs.

Broderick sagged back in his chair. He sure as hell hadn't seen that coming. Anger simmered deep in his gut. He'd let go of Glenna after one of the most memorable weekends of his life because of family loyalty. Even now, when he should be concentrating, he could almost taste her full lips... And yet he had pushed their attraction aside. He'd given everything for the Steele mantra of *Family Above All Else*.

Where was family loyalty now?

The anger kept his mouth closed tight. He didn't trust himself to speak and not say something he would later regret. His siblings had no such problems. Their shocked words tumbled on top of each other in a jumble that made it tough to gauge who said what.

Broderick pried his thoughts away from Glenna and back to the future of the Steele oil empire. "And the business leaks about stock sales? Does someone else already know about your relationship? If you've been meeting in the office, then others may already be talking. Dad, you have to know the implications to the fiscal health of both companies."

"Yes, about that..." Jack sawed into his waffles and speared a bite. "We want to work with you all on a presentation to the board for our plans to blend the companies."

Blend?

Blend the companies?

Normal businesses could blend. But this would be like combining flint and matchsticks. This was fire, an explosion—the end result possibly destroying everything they'd built.

The confirmation of Broderick's worst fear since he'd learned of those damned stock purchases stoked the flames of his anger to a full blaze. In a simple sentence, a single revelation, his father was risking what Broderick had devoted his entire adult life to preserving and growing.

"Blending the companies? As in blending everything? You can't just expect that we'll—I'll—accept that."

Jack leaned in nose to nose with his oldest son, a gesture of dominance. "That is exactly what I expect. I'm still the majority shareholder in Steele Industries, and Jeannie is majority shareholder in her company, as well. The board may have concerns. You and Glenna may have concerns. But Jeannie and I have thought this through. It's time for the feud to end. We *are* merging the companies. She and I are prepared do whatever is necessary to make that happen. You can join forces to make us a more powerful entity, or you can cash in your portion and I'll buy it at fair market value. Your choice."

"Think about what you're saying, brother," Conrad hissed in alarm, placing a hand on Jack's arm. "Are you prepared to cut out your children? Your flesh and blood?"

Broderick was wondering the same thing. If his father expected him to surrender their company without a fight, then his old man was going to be very surprised.

Jack chewed thoughtfully. "I did not say anything about cutting anyone out. I said if anyone wants to walk away from the business, they can. Family will always be welcome in my home."

Marshall spoke up. "And what about our jobs? Our family land, our heritage?"

"You're getting ahead of yourself, talking about things we haven't gotten to yet," Jack explained, looking too much at peace, considering he'd overturned their whole world. "Restructuring will create opportunities, too."

Restructuring? The word casually rolled off his tongue in the manner of someone mentioning that Alaska was cold this time of year.

The word knocked around inside Broderick's head for all of five seconds before gelling into an image that would create utter chaos for the Steeles and the Mikkelsons, both personally and professionally.

"Dad, I've given this same talk to employees on their way out the door."

His father smiled with a hard-nosed determination they'd all seen before. "Then that gives you an edge that will put you in the running to be CFO of the whole operation."

Just when Broderick thought his world couldn't be any more upended, he learned otherwise. Because his father had left no room for misunderstanding.

It was Broderick or Glenna for CFO. One of them would be ousting the other.

"I hope you don't mind that I brought my puppy."

Kneeling, Glenna nuzzled her face into the fluffy husky puppy sitting pretty in front of her. Her heart filled with tenderness for her pup, such a source of comfort and joy after her husband's death.

Feeling the weight of eyes on her, she glanced up to find Broderick studying her intently from the other side of his office. Electricity danced in the air between them.

"I don't mind a bit," he answered. "What's the little guy's name?"

"Kota. As in Dakota." She unhooked the leash and stood, monitoring Kota as he sniffed around the room. The dog sniffed the leather boots curiously. The husky pup stood at attention next to the sleek black chair, glacier-blue eyes trained on Broderick.

Clearing his throat, he walked around his desk to a minibar, pulled out a sparkling water that had been bottled locally from the Kalal glacier. The fizz and bubbles jumped around the glasses as he poured.

For a microsecond, she caught his gaze and it sent tingles down her spine, flooding her awareness. Images drifted into her mind that she knew she had to temper. This was business.

"Thank you for understanding. Kota was at doggy day care while I was at work, and even though I know he's cared for, I still want him to know me." She ruffled Kota's black-and-white head.

"He's a great pup, well behaved. You're clearly doing a good job. I don't mind at all," Broderick answered. They'd been number crunching for an hour, so far all business, leaving personal matters undiscussed.

Never in her wildest dreams would Glenna have guessed that in the span of thirty-six hours Broderick would storm back into her life again and she would then be working with him.

But that had been her mother's firm request after dropping her bombshell about the companies merging. She wanted a joint report.

"How did your meeting with your siblings and your mom go?" His whiskey-warm tones tingled through Glenna's veins like a hot toddy on a snowy day.

Glenna focused on her puppy, who was staring up at her with ice-blue eyes, trusting and pure. "Well, that's a complex question. I'm not sure we got a true read on things, since the conversation was on speakerphone. My younger brother's plane had trouble making it in from North Dakota. Everyone on the line stayed quietly civil during the news."

"That's good, though, isn't it?" Broderick said, leaning toward her.

She raised her eyebrows in answer and shrugged. "I'm cautious in saying for sure, because I fear an explosion could happen later."

In person.

And that storm would be unforgiving, filled with emotion and lengthy, loud conversations that would send the dogs and cats at the ranch house fleeing under tables and chairs.

Ice clinked and drew her attention to Broderick, who was preparing their water glasses with slices of lime. Then he dumped the candy out of a crystal dish and filled the empty bowl with the rest of the water.

The thoughtfulness, the precious gesture for her pet, melted her heart faster than sun baking a snowman. "My oldest brother, Charles, sounded calm, most likely thanks to his wife. I could tell, though, his teeth were grinding on the other end of the phone. Trystan, well, he's gruff but quiet, so who knows."

"And your baby sister?" He placed the glasses and bowl on a tray before returning to the table in the corner, not a full-out conference table, rather more of a cozy meeting area. Not nearly large enough for her liking right now.

"Alayna's a peacemaker. So unless I'm looking into her eyes, I don't know for sure." She reached for the glass, her hand brushing his. Crackles of awareness sparked along her every nerve. She took a quick swallow of water to cover her nervousness. "Thank you for this."

"I've ordered food to be brought up. If you're starving now the minibar has some granola bars—"

"This is fine. Thanks. I'll wait."

"I ordered extra. We have a long night ahead of us."

Her gaze shot to his, searching for a double entendre, but his eyes were serious tonight. None of the teasing from that first day in her office was visible.

It had been a sobering three days since then. "I'm not sure how we're supposed to do this."

She jabbed a pencil into her loose topknot. "How do we work together while protecting the interest of both companies?"

"One company, if we can take what our parents said at face value." He knelt to offer Kota the crystal bowl of water.

"I don't understand how they expect the employees to get over decades of secrecy agreements and distrust. I'm not sure how we're all supposed to get over it."

"I don't think we have a choice in the matter." The tenor of his voice struck something in her.

Only the sound of Kota lapping water and icy rain beating against the windows cut through the silence.

She drummed her fingers along the edge of her laptop, still not sure how much to share in spite of what her mother had said. But Jeannie and Jack wanted a board of directors' packet to reassure investors, and that would require Glenna and Broderick working together. "How did the meeting go with your father and your family?"

"Stunned surprise."

She lowered the laptop screen, sliding back in her leather seat. "Not a surplus of congratulations, huh?"

"We're all still in shock."

"Less than an hour after the call, my sister-in-law and baby sister started sending out texts about organizing an impromptu shower or bachelorette party or something like that for the females in both families. Made me feel bad for not jumping on board with the congrats and felicitations."

"You have to remember that they weren't blinded by the—"

"Right. Don't remind me. I feel bad about my reaction. My mother's an adult. She's entitled to her own life. It's just tough to turn on a dime and see this relationship positively, after a lifetime of our parents bad-mouthing the business practices of the other family."

He flipped a pencil over and over, tapping it on the tabletop rhythmically. She watched it linger between his fingers, mesmerized by the small, controlled gesture. Only the challenge in his voice broke her trance. "The business practices? What exactly do you object to in the way we do business?"

"I'm not trying to pick a fight." Her voice rose, and her puppy sat up, whining. "We're going to have to sort this out."

"No. We just have to come up with a cohesive plan for the financials that we can present to the board. Ways to combine assets while preserving jobs."

She snapped her fingers for Kota to come to her. "And staying on track for a pipeline."

He dovetailed on her thoughts. "Building it faster and safer, to pipe more and be competitive. It's a matter of self-preservation. Our parents haven't given us any choice."

"Right, of course." She stroked her puppy's back, the fluffy texture of his freshly washed coat soothing.

And she could definitely use all the comfort she could get right now, being closeted in this room with Broderick. Her senses were on overload from the fresh cedar scent of his aftershave, teasing and tempting her every breath. Her body wanted him... but her mind rebelled.

She still grieved for her dead husband. She'd loved him during their marriage. She'd loved him through every conflict as they'd worked so damn hard on their relationship. Yet on an earthy level, her body ached for closeness with a man. With Broderick.

Inhaling, she shivered at the delicious tingle of his scent even as she resented the tightening of her nipples. "Do you ever want more than…this? The job, the office?"

"No," he answered without hesitation. "Does that mean you do want more? What would that be?"

Was it just her wayward imagination or had his voice lowered to an intimate level on that last question? His eyes locked on hers with a heat that seared right through her.

Her heart slugged faster in her chest even as she fought for composure. A professional distance.

"Oh, you're not getting rid of me that easily. My job's not up for grabs." She pulled the pen from her hair and pointed it his way. "And neither am I."

She needed to remind herself as much as she needed to tell him.

Hands off Broderick Steele, she reminded herself.

"Why not? The wall's been torn down." He gave her a truly quizzical look, as if he was genuinely considering the idea and not just flirting.

Something about his tone made her wary. And very, very hot.

She breathed deep, too aware of her body's every response to this man.

"No, no, stop right there. From the minute you walked in my office door three days ago, you've been filling what you say with sexual overtones." She had to halt this line of discussion before she started questioning if maybe he had a point. "Now more than ever, sex between us would complicate things."

"How so?" That sly grin formed dimples in his cheeks.

"You're smarter than that." She looked down, shaking her head while pretending to scrutinize his boots. "We don't need to add more tension to an already strained situation. We're not college students who've had a bit too much to drink at a party."

"You're right. We're not rebellious kids. We're adults who know exactly what's going on. Our parents are getting married. We'll likely have to share Christmas dinner year after year. That's a fact." He leaned closer to her, across the table. His musky scent mingled with the playful growl in his voice. "But there's always the mistletoe."

At the mention of such a cozy scene, the fire in her belly cooled. The image he painted was too... personal. "This isn't funny. You're sexy as hell, and clearly, I'm attracted to you. But I've lost enough. I'm not going to risk losing my job and my family, too."

"I like hearing that the attraction is mutual." He twined his fingers with hers on top of her puppy.

"Again, I will say, you're a smart man. You had to know." Her fingers curled for an instant before she pulled away.

"I didn't, not for sure. You made a hasty run for the door all those years ago after what I thought was an incredible weekend."

"It was...memorable," she said, then rushed to add, "in a good way. But we can both see now how difficult that would have been. Think how impossible it feels to have your dad marry my mom. How tough would it have been back then after that impulsive weekend to combat our families' feuds?"

"And after that you got married." A flatness entered his voice.

"Yes, I did." She tipped her chin defiantly, then tried to lighten the mood. "And you have to admit your reputation as a ladies' man is well earned. Those tabloid articles can't be all rumor."

"The gossips are going to be busy enough right now with my father and your mother. I don't think they'll have time left over for the two of us." He skimmed his knuckles along her cheek in a flash of sensation before returning to his computer. "Think about it."

There was no missing the invitation in his eyes. The attraction echoed inside her. And as lonely as she'd been, her body ached for the simple touch of a man. This man.

But no.

With Broderick, it would be more than a touch.

And it would never be simple.

Four

Jack Steele had known it would be tough getting his offspring and Jeannie's adult children on board with merging their two warring companies. But hell's bells, he hadn't expected such a massive wall of bull-headed resistance.

His redwood mansion in the distance now, he settled deeper into the saddle, hoping the quarter horse's rhythmic gait crunching through snow would settle his frustration. Riding had saved him from losing his cool more than once. In fact, riding had saved his sanity after his wife and daughter died in that plane crash. The open sky was his sanctuary, day or night.

Right now, the sun glistened off the snowcapped trees and mountains. Glistened off Jeannie's hair as she rode beside him. He'd dreamed of taking her horseback riding once they could be seen in public together. Another reason he should be happy, but the world was topsy-turvy.

Jack gripped the reins loosely in his hands. He'd saddled up the Paint—Willow—for Jeannie. She was a natural. Just as he'd known she would be. The sunshine brought out the lighter shades in her golden hair, which was slipping free from the hood of her parka. She perched confidently in the saddle, the gentle curves of her slim body calling to him. The cinched waist of her parka. Her long legs that made him think of how much he would enjoy tugging off her boots, her jeans and silk leggings.

He would never forget that moment six months ago when they'd found themselves alone at a business conference in Juneau. He'd looked at her. She'd looked at him.

And the world had changed.

He'd felt it. Seen it echoed in her eyes. He'd asked her to have a drink with him. She'd said yes...and here they were. Together. Committed.

Clearing his throat with a breath of icy air, he returned his attention to the present. To the ride. His first with Jeannie. He could envision many more such outings in their future.

Once they settled the controversy between their children.

Damn it all. He scrubbed his gloved hand under the lamb's wool collar of his coat. He and Jeannie were adults, for God's sake. Their spouses had died years ago. He wasn't ready to crawl in the grave, not by a longshot.

Maybe if he'd found someone else, someone without the surname Mikkelson… But life had always thrown him curve balls, and apparently, his love life wasn't any different. Knowing how precious happiness was made him all the more determined to enjoy what he'd found.

He glanced at Jeannie as she swayed alongside him, so regally beautiful she threatened to steal his breath all over again. "Thank you for coming today, to my home."

She smiled back at him. "Our home, soon."

"That it will be." He still couldn't believe she'd agreed to leave her own home for his. "We could build a place of our own, if you wish, or if you think it would make things easier for your children."

She scanned the stretch of land from his sprawling mansion to the seaplane bobbing on the lake. "This place is lovely. I promise I'll be slow in putting my own stamp on things so as not to upset the Steele applecart."

"It's your home, too," he said firmly. "Your choices are mine."

Her exhalations puffed a cloud of white into the afternoon air. "If only it could be that simple. Are you sure you're prepared for this fight? For what it could cost us?"

"Nothing in life has come easily for me or mine. My children are made of tougher stuff. Once they get past the surprise—"

"Shock," Jeannie corrected.

"Well, that's one way of putting it." He couldn't hold back his chuckle at the memory of Broderick's and Glenna's faces when they'd opened that bathroom door. "They certainly didn't learn in the gradual way we'd planned."

Jeannie laughed along with him, the sound of their voices floating together on the wind. Damn, he was getting downright poetic these days.

Love did that to a man.

He reached for the reins to Jeannie's horse and guided both animals to a stop. He reached out to stroke back Jeannie's hair and tuck it into her hood, then cupped her neck. "What we've found together is a gift."

Her blue eyes glistened with tears and she touched his wrist, squeezing. "One I didn't expect to have again."

"And one I'm not giving up," he said without hesitation.

"Even if it threatens your business?"

"Even if it threatens yours?"

"Ours," she answered with a smile. "Like the houses."

"Exactly." He slid his hand down to grip her waist, then lifted her from the horse and onto his lap.

"We are a team now." She looped her arms around his neck, leaning against him. "This is real."

"Yes, my dear, it is very real." As real as his growing need to have her right now. But this was more than an affair. He loved her. "Our families need to get on board with our engagement. No more separate explanations, separate family meetings. They have to learn how to be together if the business merger stands a chance at working."

"You're right." She kissed him once, twice, enticing as hell. "And the sooner the better. For them as well as for us, because I love you, Jack Steele."

"I know you do. I love you, too, lady." He hugged her closer, securing both sets of reins in his fist. "And you know what else?"

"Do tell?"

"I want you. Right now."

And lucky for them, the plane hangar was very, very close.

Glenna clutched the edge of her chair. She was in the glassed-in sunroom at the Steele family lodge for their first big co-family gathering. It was so surreal.

Not that it was a completely blended family get-together. The women sat on different sides of the room, based on family affiliation. Glenna and Alayna stayed closer to their mother, along with their sister-in-law, Shana. Whereas the two Steele hostesses, Naomi and Delaney, stood like bookends near the wet bar, so alike in appearance even if opposite in temperament, Naomi being a partying wild spirit, Delaney an intensely serious green-issues crusader.

The men were outside, horseback riding on a sunny day that melted snow into a glistening display. It could have been a gathering at Glenna's mother's home—her parents' home—except more than double the people were present.

Through the window she could see her two brothers riding expertly alongside the five Steele men. But Broderick drew her eyes most today, his Stetson a hint higher than the others since he was so tall. His collar was flipped up, with the lamb's wool against his ears. His hand held the reins loosely, confidently.

Broderick's bay quarter horse, Abacus, demanded nearly as much attention as his rider. They were a matched set. Dark, muscular—commanding. Even the way the bay tossed his mane said something of his wild, albeit tempered, nature. The two moved like one, almost as if Broderick's soul had been fused to the bay. Every response, every turn seemed to happen from instinct.

Was there anything this man couldn't handle?

Glenna's hand dropped to Kota, stroking the puppy's fur for comfort. Each touch of his coat soothed her ragged nerves.

She'd thought about Broderick's proposition again and again throughout the night. But they weren't two strangers meeting for the first time, with no entanglements. He had to understand they couldn't just resume where they'd left off long ago.

But if she *were* meeting him for the first time?

Her gaze wandered back to the sight of him tall and strong on horseback. Her stomach lurched with awareness—and apprehension.

Yes, even if she were meeting him for the first time right now, she would still run. Because truth be told, this attraction was more than she could risk.

Her emotions had to be off-limits. Losing her husband had already decimated her heart.

Glenna drew her attention back to the rustic luxury of the sunroom, a room that was the direct opposite of the Steeles' sleek office space. Fat leather chairs and sofas filled the expansive, light-filled room. Rafters soared upward, dotted with skylights, as well as lantern-style lights for the long winter nights. One stone wall held a fireplace crackling with flames. Elk antlers hung above the mantel. The wet bar was laden with snacks and drinks.

The room was packed with wary women, gathered at the edict of Jeannie and Jack.

Glenna's sister-in-law, Shana shot to her feet. "We're going to play a party game. I reached out to Naomi and we've come up with some icebreakers to help us all—" she gestured weakly "—get over the *newness* of this."

Well now, wasn't that diplomatic? Kudos to Shana.

Jeannie waved from a log-style rocking chair. "Please, not one of those wedding shower games where we all end up wearing silly hats covered with bows."

Glenna's baby sister winced. "Or please say we don't have to tell lies and truths and guess. I never win those because people can always tell when I'm lying."

Edgy, Naomi stood, wearing brown leather leggings with a thick Sherpa vest. "We're going to play the dating game."

Alayna frowned, peering around the room at each

woman. "But she's already engaged, and she's already married, and I suspect that she—"

"No," Naomi stated, "this is a different sort of dating game. I've been consulting with a company that helps people write their bios for online dating sites—"

Her sister chuckled. "You've done *what*?"

"You heard me, Delaney. Guys in particular have a tough time expressing themselves with words, so they ask for help. It's like marketing or editing. I have some samples and we're going to figure out who's for real and who's a poser."

Shana gathered her thick caramel-colored mane and tossed it over her shoulders. "Like the kind of guy who hangs out in a bar and claims to be an astronaut."

"Great example." Naomi walked to a corner table with the laptop computer connected to three wide screen televisions. "The names have been changed to protect the guys. Now are we ready to play the game?"

A dating game? Glenna would rather do the polar bear plunge, jumping naked into icy water. But she said, "Let's get started." So they would be done all the sooner and she could go home, away from this awkward gathering and the tempting view of Broderick as his horse galloped along the fence line.

Shana clapped her hands. "Good. Here are the rules. One point for every warning sign, five points if you can catch an outright lie."

Delaney's expression said she was clearly not sold yet. Glenna wasn't, either; her eyes kept returning to the window, to the wild scenery and the precision with which Broderick moved with his horse.

"I was thinking for each correct guess, pick your poison for someone or yourself—a champagne Jell-O shot or a chocolate truffle?" Shana suggested.

Forcing herself back into the present moment, Glenna decided to be helpful. "Where are the truffles and alcohol?"

Naomi and Shana each swept a silver cover off a platter just as the wide screen televisions hummed to life. Each TV went to split screen, with multiple profiles.

"Oh, oh!" Her cousin Sage's hand shot into the air. "Well, this is easy enough. I see five guys with creepster in their profile name. Like 'Legman.' Four guys reference their penis length."

"Eww." Alayna shook her head. "And there are two with 'hard' in their name." Both she and Sage rushed to the minibar and popped an assortment of champagne Jell-O shots and truffles into their mouths. They savored them with closed eyes, *yums* and *mmms*.

Glenna crossed her arms tightly over her chest. "Do guys really think we go for that level of slime?" She pointed to another screen. "The guys on the left side appear real."

Yes, for the moment, she would play this game and drink a little champagne, then she'd be on her way.

Her eyes went to Broderick again. She wasn't in any condition to be in the same room with him once the men came back inside. She'd spent so much time with him this week, she couldn't handle being in this house with him surrounded by family. It was too close to the cozy mistletoe image he'd painted for her back in his office.

Naomi nodded. "Well done, future stepsister. Help yourself to the treats."

Stepsister? Glenna made a beeline for the champagne shots. Another mark on the why-anything-with-Broderick would be infinitely complicated. The sweet, slippery shot with a kick sent a delicious tingle along her senses. Yes. Just what she needed. This would be her treat of choice for the duration of the game.

Especially if she expected to get through an evening with Broderick and keep her sanity.

"I'm sure there are good ones out there, too. Honest ones." Glenna considered another shot, just for the hell of it.

"We could do a percentage chart of how many there are, and I'm guessing it will all average out. The point here is to be wise, ladies. Be wise."

Naomi snorted. "Or stay single."

Shana laughed. "Cynic."

"Realist." Naomi waved to the minibar. "Please help yourself to the food before the men return."

"What?" Alayna stood, swaying a little, clearly a drinking lightweight. "That's it?"

"Would you have preferred a male stripper?" Naomi's laugh was hoarse and deep. Genuine. Glenna liked her honesty.

"Let it be known for the record," Naomi continued, winking with playful mischief that almost hid the tension in her face, a tension echoed in all of them at this forced gathering. "I would have voted for a stripper, a cowboy. Or at the very least a lingerie shower, but your sister-in-law shot down those ideas."

Shana shrugged. "I wasn't sure Jeannie would approve. Now, let's enjoy this amazing food. The Steeles' chef is truly exceptional I have to say. Jeannie? A Jell-O shot?"

Jeannie shook her head, her shoulder-length hair brushing her shoulders in a blond-gray echo of her children's coloring.

Alayna stumbled over and gripped her mother's arm. "You're not pregnant, are you, Mom? Do we need to have a talk with you before the wedding?"

Glenna's thoughts winged back to the night before her own wedding. Her mom and sisters had gathered around her as they ate ice cream and watched chick flicks. Nostalgia and regret rolled over her.

Jeannie patted Alayna's hand, dismissive and amused. The matriarch winked. "I think I've got that covered."

"Clearly." Glenna's mind skipped over the images of that fateful walk in and moved right to memories of a similar shower moment with Broderick back in college. God, she needed to speed this party along, snag her coat and leave. "Perhaps you could give us some notes—"

The burgeoning camaraderie was cut short by a swelling of voices outside. Louder and louder, even shouting. Glenna shot to her feet, searching through the windows. The men were sliding from their horses beside a Range Rover. A young woman stood beside the car, holding a baby swaddled in a pink parka.

Curiosity brought Glenna to the edge of her seat, her eyes drawn to that precious bundle. Murmurs filled the sunroom, but Glenna only half heard. Her gaze was still trained beyond the windows. Before she could question the wisdom of her action, she stood and reached for her white wool coat and cashmere scarf.

Two guards raced from the fence line, closing in on the group of men dismounting.

Inside, the other women at the party gathered up their coats, too, without a break in their buzz of chatter, but Glenna led the pack, being the closest to the exit. She tugged on her coat and pulled open the door. A blast of crisp air washed over her.

Voices carried on the breeze.

"Ma'am." Conrad held up two hands. "I've never touched you."

What the hell? Glenna's eyes shifted back to the baby, her heart aching as it always did when she saw a child, given the loss of so many pregnancies. She'd never even made it to the second trimester. Never felt life move inside her.

The stranger jostled the baby on her hip and fished an envelope from her jacket pocket. "I'm not little Fleur's mother. I work for Mr. Steele—the senior Mr. Steele. Someone—I don't know how—left the baby in the barn and I found her while I was refilling the food and water troughs for your return. Security is still trying to figure out how the baby was brought in. But there was a note on top of her…"

Jack took the envelope from her hand, glanced at the outside. Blinking fast, he looked sharply at Broderick, then Glenna, giving only a moment's heart-stopping warning before he announced, "It's addressed to Broderick...and Glenna."

Five

Glenna's stomach clenched as Jack read the outside of the envelope…addressed to her and Broderick?

Gasps rippled through the family crowded around her, sending puffs into the cold air. She glanced at Broderick, but found no answers on his handsome face. He looked as puzzled as she felt. He rubbed his temple, just under the brim of his Stetson.

Glenna pulled her gaze away from his strong, beard-stubbled jaw. What did this child have to do with her? With both of them? Even as she thought the question, she couldn't help but reach for the little bundle in a pink parka and a blanket. The sweet weight settling into her arms was a precious, squirming joy. Her heart swelled. She stroked a knuckle along the cherub's cheek. Wide blue eyes blinked up at her, the tiny mouth sucking on a pacifier.

She felt Broderick step up behind her, his boots crunching through the snow. She glanced back to see him look over her shoulder at the baby, then over at Jack, who was still staring at the letter.

Glenna hugged the child closer, the pink blanket trailing from her arms. "What does the note say?"

The paper crackled as Jack handed it back to the secretary who handled it carefully, as if preserving evidence, and then withdrew a sheet of paper. A swirly scrawl filled the pristine white surface. "Um, sir…" The woman from the barn passed the paper to Jack Steele. "You may want to read this. I'm not comfortable with, um, well…"

A hint of snow started whispering from the sky as Jack took the paper and then pulled a second typed document from the envelope, scanning both while tipping them for Jeannie to see. "The note says she isn't sure who the baby's father is," he reported. "She sent a birth certificate for a three-month-old baby named Fleur Wilson. It lists the mother's name as Deborah Wilson…"

Jack looked over his glasses at his oldest son and Broderick's eyebrows shot up. Tellingly so. Glenna swallowed hard. The name was unfamiliar to her, though.

Jack glanced down, swiped a few snowflakes from his glasses and continued. "She goes on to write there's no use in looking for her. She's already in Canada and will contact us when she's ready. But for now, she wants her child to be with family." He cleared his throat. "Her message says she isn't sure if the father is Broderick or…"

Jeannie rested a hand on his shoulder, took the papers and walked over to her daughter, worry was stamped across the older woman's face. "Glenna, the note says the father could also be Gage. I'm sorry to even have to say that out loud."

Glenna bit back a gasp. Her dead husband could be the father of this child?

Even with the gentle voice of her mother delivering the words, Glenna felt the blow of each syllable in her gut. She gasped in a gulp of the crisp air, swaying and forcing to herself to hold on to the baby more securely. She felt the weight of so many eyes on her, this strange mix of family and long-time enemies as she processed news that threatened to bring her to her knees.

Silence reigned, as if the group held their collective breath. Behind her, she heard the snort and stamp of one of the horses.

In some distant part of her consciousness, she realized that Broderick had placed a steadying hand on her waist. Surely he had to be staggering at this revelation, too. She looked into the baby's face, searching the features for a magic clue to the parentage. She eased back the baby's hood and knit cap to find light brown hair. No real clue there. She shielded the tiny face with her hand to keep the snowflakes from landing.

It seemed the more she stared at the infant, the more this little girl became her own person. With each passing second, her face became more distinctly different from Gage's or Broderick's.

Glenna shook her head while swaying to rock the baby. The swishing movement calmed her as much as it did the little babe. With a slow exhalation, she said, "It's okay." The words steadied her. "Don't tiptoe around or worry about what needs to be said. The most important thing is that we focus on this child and making sure she's safe and healthy."

Broderick nodded tightly. "We should contact the police. She could be a kidnapped child."

"Oh, God," Glenna gasped, and studied the baby's face again. Such innocence, unaware of the chaos in her world. Thank God. "I never considered that possibility. We should check with the authorities."

Broderick's brother Marshall—the middle Steele son—took the papers from Jeannie. "I'll meet with our security team here and we'll contact the police. We can find out if there are missing child alerts, and let them know the baby is here."

"Thank you, son," Jack said.

Glenna's mind began to clear. "We should go inside where it's warm and dry. We also need to make sure she has fresh formula." She found comfort in taking control as she charged toward the towering redwood mansion. "I'm assuming the note doesn't say when she ate last. She could be hungry any moment now, and she's been through enough change without having to be uncomfortable for even an instant."

Broderick scooped up a pink checkered diaper bag and walked beside her. "Apparently, she came with this." He unzipped the sack. "It looks like there are some of her things inside."

What was he thinking right now? This could be his child. Had that registered with him? Glenna couldn't envision him as a single father.

Truly, she couldn't envision much of anything at the moment. "I'm not sure I trust anything dropped off by a stranger who dumped her baby with people the poor little tyke has never met. At least we can use the formula brand to go shopping." She climbed the wooden steps to the back deck of the Steele mansion, all too aware of Broderick's bracing hand on her back. A steadying and unsettling assurance all at once. "Bottom line, this baby is an innocent and she needs our help."

Her thoughts winged fast to the reality of sharing this baby with Broderick, even for a short time. She couldn't help but feel the strength of his touch, and yes, a tingle of awareness where each of his fingers settled on her back. He would make a powerful partner for a woman.

And she couldn't deny that seeing him in this new light was flipping her world upside down.

Broderick paced around the lodge's great room.

Even in this expansive space, he felt caged in, waiting for Glenna to join him with the baby…

The baby.

Potentially *his* baby.

Fleur.

He didn't know what he thought about the possibility of being a father. Of what this would mean for his attraction to Glenna or the fact that he wanted to pursue her even in the middle of family drama.

He couldn't help but think about the possessiveness he'd felt earlier when he'd placed his arm around Glenna. Seeing the way she cradled the child—possibly *his* child—had burned through him with a fierceness that rattled him even now.

Each successive lap on the thick rug brought more questions, more unease.

Every stable aspect of his life had been yanked from him in a very short time.

Boots thudding off the carpet, Broderick made his way to the stone fireplace. Flames danced along the logs, casting orange-tinged shadows in the room lit only by a small table lamp.

A stranger walking in would mistake the space as soothing and luxurious. But right now, tension hummed so palpably through Broderick that he was sure it filled the space around him.

And he wasn't sure how to fix the world again.

He paused in front of the fireplace, kneeling to stoke the flames to a crackling blaze. One of the logs settled with a shower of sparks.

Hungry for normalcy, he surveyed the room. The fireplace wall was dominated by massive moose antlers—a family heirloom that had belonged to his great-grandfather when Steele Industries was just getting started. Back when Alaska was a wilderness to be conquered. Tall ceilings normally provided an airy balance to the thick leather sofas that filled the room, but did nothing to alleviate the pressure and confusion jackhammering in Broderick's mind.

Pacing again, he wandered with determined footfalls to the other side of the room, to a painting of an Alaskan forest. He was no art aficionado, but he appreciated the vivid colors and strong brushstrokes that seemed to capture so perfectly the nuance of light in early springtime.

Some of the family had gone with Glenna's sister-in-law to the store to get supplies for the baby. Other members were in the kitchen putting together food for the adults, as the evening threatened to stretch beyond the hours allotted for the party. His father and his father's *fiancée*, a word Broderick still had to get used to associating with Jeannie, had given Glenna and Broderick the chance to speak privately. Here, in this room, where he was waiting and pacing.

Raking his hand through his hair, he let out a sigh at the exact moment he heard the door click open.

Spinning around, he saw Glenna, baby in tow.

Damn.

Glenna was always stunning. For as long as he had known her, her slender frame and bright eyes had drawn him in. As did her intelligence and generosity. All the layers that made her Glenna were undeniably attractive.

But seeing her with the baby sent his heart pounding. This was a softer side of Glenna he'd never glimpsed up close before. A tender, nurturing side that made him… damn. He didn't know. He'd never been with a woman who looked like that.

In his gut, he felt a stirring. He wanted to protect his potential child.

And Glenna.

Her smooth voice interrupted his staring. "Fleur's calmer now, and I imagine once she eats she'll sleep for the night."

Sitting in a plush padded rocking chair, she settled herself with the baby. A heavy sigh slid from Glenna's lips as she gave him a weary but valiant smile.

Broderick crossed to the sofa adjacent to her, his leg brushing hers. Even with the barrier of his jeans and her wool slacks, he could still remember the feel of her skin. A hint of her almond scent teased his senses and threatened to distract him, making him want to lean closer and inhale.

And now wasn't that distracting as hell?

He gathered his thoughts and sat. "I think we're all in agreement that you and I need to talk." He glanced at his boots, the leather still damp from his ride earlier. The world had gone haywire in less time than it took water to evaporate. "As awkward as this is, we need to know what we're facing, depending on whose child this is."

The weight of those words hit Broderick as he fully realized how awful this had to be for Glenna. He'd been so wrapped up in his own shock, he hadn't thought about how hurtful this had to be for her. "God, Glenna. I'm sorry. This has to be painful for you. I assume since you haven't shut this paternity question down altogether, there's a possibility the baby is Gage's?"

Her brow furrowing, she shook her head, a whisper of blond hair escaping her loose topknot and grazing her cheek. "I don't know for sure. We were having a…rough patch. It's not…impossible that she could be his. But I have no knowledge of her and he certainly never mentioned any pregnancy."

Her eyes looked past him, drifting to the painting of the Alaskan forest. A moment of weariness flashed over her face, but he watched her quickly gather her composure, a skill developed in boardroom meetings. Her attention returned to the baby. Smiling again, she rocked the tiny girl gently.

"I'm sorry about the problems you and your husband had." And he was. If this was indeed Gage's child…

"Me, too. But you can tuck away your pity for me and save it for Fleur." Glenna looked up from the baby. "And you? You didn't shout 'hell no, not my kid.'"

"It's possible." He had to admit it. "I met Deborah Wilson when she came up here to do a series of articles on the likelihood of us pursuing a pipeline. She and I went out. It wasn't serious. But there is a possibility. Not probable, since I was only with her once and we, um, used protection. But then nothing's one hundred percent except abstinence."

"Then she could be yours." Glenna bobbed her head up and down, her loose topknot glimmering in the warm light.

He gave her a sidelong glance, weighing his words, but knowing he needed to share what was on his mind. "We went out a few times, but I ended it when she broke down in tears telling me she was involved with a married man."

There were some lines he did not cross. He might not want marriage for himself, but he still believed firmly in the sanctity of the union. Even when dating, he stayed monogamous for the duration of that relationship.

Glenna inhaled sharply. "You believe that married man was my husband."

"I didn't say that." He reached across to touch her elbow, to comfort her. "I'm only saying this baby is here, and there's a chance she's family."

Family to one of them. That alone was enough.

His touch lingered, and he found himself unable to pull away.

"And we have to watch over her until we know..." Glenna rocked gently. "If Fleur is my husband's child and Deborah Wilson has given up her rights, then I could be a potential guardian, legally. Right? Because if he had lived, this would be my stepchild." The pronouncement was filled with logic, acceptance and generosity. Everything that made her so damn attractive to him. But he knew they needed to slow this down.

"That's a complicated issue, Glenna, with a lot of ifs—"

"But possible." Her interjection betrayed her determination. Looking back at the baby, she leaned forward to kiss the tiny pink forehead and smooth the whispery hair.

And just like that, the tender gesture made him feel

as if he had walked in on a private moment. As if he was seeing a side of Glenna no one but him had ever witnessed—one she perhaps would not want him to see.

He cleared his throat. "The word of the night. *Possible*. She could be my child and I will operate from that perspective starting now. I won't have her ever thinking I wasn't her champion." He and Glenna would figure this out. But if this was his child, he would be there for his daughter.

"I'm not sure I trust you to mix formula."

A smile twitched his lips. He raised his brows high. "I can do fractions."

"Can you burp a baby and change diapers?"

He shrugged. "I can find a sitter."

"Or we can work together." Her eyes were glassy in the muted light, but still fierce. The question of paternity meant neither of them would relinquish the child.

The idea settled in him, the rightness of the solution. Working with her to care for Fleur would only further his goal of pursuing Glenna. Yet even as he thought of the advantages, he forced himself to keep things light so as not to scare her off.

"Are you propositioning me?" he teased.

Snorting on a laugh, she shifted in the rocking chair, lightly patting the baby's bottom. "With baby puke on my shoulder?" She winked, her mouth smiling but her eyes still holding a hint of hurt, fear. "Sure."

"Damn, you're making me remember why I liked you."

"I'm sure I can make you forget just as quickly."

He knelt beside her, avoiding her challenge and truly studying the baby for the first time. How was it he didn't know somehow if this was his child?

Regardless, he felt protective toward the innocent life. "She will have the full weight of my protection."

Glenna's face knotted briefly in surprise. But as soon as their eyes met, a cord tightened between them. He felt it in his stomach, knew that he had to have her, convince her. Even amid all these complications...

There was something tangible between them.

His cell phone chimed, a loud ding that knocked his gaze away.

Broderick bit back a hiss of frustration and pulled out his phone. "That's my dad. They've got formula for the baby, a nurse practitioner...and an attorney, my sister Naomi, who's speaking with the police."

As the early Alaska dark settled, Glenna realized she and Broderick had unexpectedly joined forces.

They had both positioned chairs by the new portable crib. Fleur snoozed with a full stomach, oblivious to the massive changes going on around her.

The house was stocked with baby gear and food. The nurse had checked the baby over and she appeared healthy. The police had determined there were no missing child alerts that matched Fleur. The birth certificate had been registered, and an APB on Deborah Wilson's car had turned up that she had indeed crossed into Canada. Beyond that, she'd disappeared.

Which left Glenna and Broderick as this baby's only possible family.

Broderick's sister Naomi was a fierce lawyer. Sure, she had a brilliant legal mind, but she was also a bit ruthless and certainly didn't sugarcoat a thing.

Naomi's eyes narrowed as she spoke to them. "Let me talk to a friend of mine in child services. There are so many children in the system… Given that you're willing to admit possible paternity, we'll try for a temporary guardianship until the matter can be settled with DNA tests. If you're amenable. Glenna, the lab can use something of your husband's, like an old hairbrush, or perhaps his mother once saved his baby teeth…"

Glenna's already overloaded mind balked at Naomi taking over in such a complete fashion. Suspicion inched up Glenna's spine. Her mom might trust the Steele family, but that didn't mean Glenna was on board with letting a former business rival make choices for her life. Naomi was a well-known shark and her loyalty would be to her own family. "Temporary guardianship? For which one of us?"

"Just what it sounds like. While you two were talking, I chatted with Dad and Jeannie. And since none of us could envision either of you two backing down, we thought it would be best for the two of you to take care of the baby together until we sort this out— paternity and legalities."

Broderick bristled. "That leaves the baby and all of us open to more gossip at a time when there's already enough going on."

Glenna turned to stare him down, her softer feelings toward him starting to evaporate. So much for unity. "You're really worrying about the company right now? This has nothing to do with business."

Broderick held up a hand. "The way I see it, the less negative gossip about our families the better for Fleur if this goes to some kind of custody battle."

Warning bells sounded in Glenna's mind. She knew the Steele family was a force to be reckoned with. But they could stuff their take-charge attitude. This baby could well be tied to her. It could be a tie to her husband—a reminder that their marriage had been troubled, yes, but also an answer to her prayers for a child she could love as her own. She wasn't giving up even a few days with the baby. "I'm not leaving. I won't be pushed out of Fleur's life—"

Broderick touched her elbow again in that comforting way that also launched butterflies in her stomach. "What if we care for her together, somewhere outside of the Steele or Mikkelson backyards, so the baby isn't a distraction from the merger?"

Naomi nodded curtly. "I have to agree with my pigheaded brother on this. Speaking as a part of this family-company-merger mess, I think getting away is best for the two of you, as well. You'll have the quiet you'll need to sort out the financial side of blending our businesses, to figure out what to present to the board. It benefits all of us if the two of you mend personal fences."

All eyes focused on them with a new intensity.

Glenna raised her eyebrows. "Personal fences? You can't possibly expect us to fix the family feud."

"Don't play coy with us. I'm not talking about the Steele-Mikkelson battle. Neither one of you is fooling me." This must be that famous courtroom face that Naomi wore to win her most difficult cases. "I went to the same college and was only a couple of years behind you. I heard. I know."

Broderick straightened his spine. "Naomi. Stand down. This most certainly isn't the time or place and it definitely isn't any of your business."

She flicked her long brown hair over her shoulder, not in the least intimidated. "I'm not a gossip. But I am smart and I see the wisdom of getting the hell out of Dodge. The wisest thing for you two to do now? Make the most of the window of time I can get you with a temporary custody order while DNA tests are run and a search is made for the child's mother. Use that time to figure out how to get along and settle our companies' business. Take your own advice, Broderick, and lie low."

The words sank in. Hard. And Glenna couldn't ignore the wisdom of Naomi's plan.

Which meant she would be stuck playing house, alone with this baby she already loved…and Broderick.

Six

Cold light reflected on the pristine shore of the Steele family compound an hour outside of Anchorage. The rays bounced up at Broderick in an unforgiving manner. Reaching for his sunglasses tucked into his shirt pocket, he breathed in the crisp air, enjoying the frigid burst against his lungs.

For his whole life, he'd been taught the importance of family. As he surveyed the distant snowcapped peaks from his spot on the runway behind the family compound, his desire to protect this place—and what might be his infant daughter—filled him.

With a bag slung over his back, he made his way to the seaplane bobbing alongside the dock. Two pontoons kept it afloat. Last year, they'd invested in the modified amphibious aircraft version that could take off and land on either water or runways. That choice made sense for flexibility, and was a benefit now, with Glenna and the baby, if an emergency arose.

The blue of the water intensified next to the piercing white of the plane, looking more like a painting than reality. The rustic mansion on the hill seemed to demand that he act now to save his family's legacy. He gave a cursory glance to a smaller, pale yellow aircraft peeking out of the hangar. He preferred that twin engine plane, but the floatplane was more practical for where he and Glenna were headed.

Together. With a baby.

They would be staying at a Steele family cabin along a secluded bay on Prince William Sound in the Gulf of Alaska. The two-bedroom A-frame with a sizable loft had served as a welcome retreat anytime one of his family members needed to recharge.

He flipped up the collar on his coat, the wind pulling so hard today he'd opted for a cap rather than his Stetson. Hopefully the crosswinds would ease up soon so he could fly the aircraft out on schedule.

He and Glenna would be alone together, plotting the financial future of their families' combined companies and caring for a tiny baby. And yes, the thought of taking care of that infant made him nervous. He didn't know a damn thing about babies. Still, he knew he needed to learn, especially if this child turned out to be his.

A possibility that still stole his breath.

Hoisting an oversize suitcase onto the seaplane, he felt his muscles strain. They had packed formula and baby supplies, all collected within two hours of the baby's arrival. These next few days would be challenging.

From the corner of his eye, Broderick saw his father help Glenna into the plane, then hand her the baby carrier. Not that he'd ever been a gambler, but this scene was not one he'd ever thought he'd witness.

A whip of Alaskan wind tore across the dock, ruffling the pale pink blanket draped over the carrier. Next, his father hoisted Kota's crate up into the plane. Kota's intense blue eyes regarded every movement with curiosity. Broderick's brother Marshall checked the instruments, making sure the plane would get to the cabin safely.

Broderick clapped his father on the shoulder as Marshall left the craft, stepping onto the dock beside them. "Thank you for your help finishing up here. And pass along my thanks for all the shopping and packing up of supplies."

Marshall passed along a travel mug of coffee. "No worries, brother. The plane's fueled and everything checks out. I even took her up for a spin this morning."

"I appreciate that."

Jack shifted his weight, straightening his puffed insulated jacket. "I called the service. The cabin has been aired out and stocked with food. The heat's been turned on."

"Thanks, Dad."

A full smile pushed up his father's mustache. "Anything the three of you need, just let me know. We'll send it up."

"I need you to let me know if you and Jeannie change your minds. You're sending me off to review our company's financials with our biggest business rival. And to be fair, Jeannie Mikkelson is asking Glenna to do the same. Be one hundred percent certain this is what you want."

"Son, we have to stay united and strong. Otherwise, our competition will gain traction during this time of transition. We're all family now. I'm certain this is what I want." Jack hauled Broderick in for a back-thumping hug before stepping away. "Now get to work."

"Yes, sir." He'd been given his marching orders in clear terms. And to be frank, he was looking forward to this time with Glenna. Maybe he could figure out this tenacious attraction between them. Maybe they could put their feelings to rest, find peace. The baby only made the stakes higher. They needed to find common ground so they could move forward as a blended Steele and Mikkelson company—and family.

Broderick stepped onto the plane, his eyes immediately finding Glenna. Somehow, she managed to look radiant strapped in the backseat, attentively bent over Fleur, cooing reassurances. The smells of cold air, pine and salt drifted into the cabin on a gust of wind. This might be a turbulent ride.

Kota let out a quiet whine beside Glenna from the secured crate, tail wagging in hopes of some attention.

She looked natural, sitting between a baby and a puppy, her hair pulled back into a loose bun. She seemed to notice Broderick's gaze, because her blue eyes met his. He gave her a curt nod and smile, then continued to the front of the plane to check the equipment himself in spite of his brother's assurances. Safety was too important.

While strapping himself into the pilot's seat, he glanced at Glenna and Fleur again, enjoying the sight of them from his mirror. He had to focus. He settled his headset into a good fit and felt the rush of pre-flight squarely in his stomach, right up until he accelerated the plane. The drumroll before being airborne had always thrilled him. He longed for the feeling when the craft lifted from ground or sea and found life in the air.

As he saw the panorama unfold before him, his breath caught. Untamed wilderness flooded his vision.

He felt connected to the wild land in his home state—an heir to tenacity and resilience. Off to the left, he saw a herd of caribou galloping in the spring sunshine.

Broderick called over his shoulder, "We're level now if you would like to move forward and talk." He studied her in the rearview mirror. "Looks like the munchkin is sleeping hard. You can watch her in the mirror up here."

Glenna worried her bottom lip, then reached for her seat belt. "Sure, we could get started on work."

Or they could talk.

Yes, they were here for Fleur and for their families, but he also needed to use every moment of this time together to figure out his attraction to Glenna.

If the opportunity presented itself, he wanted back in her bed. Because his desire for her messed with his thinking at a time when he needed clear focus.

The plane hit a pocket of air, bobbling for an instant, then settling. He latched on to Fleur as a topic that could open an honest dialogue with Glenna about how they would move forward. "Looks like Fleur is sleeping well. She's a cute little munchkin, for sure."

Glenna didn't immediately respond, but when she did her words hit him with an emotional punch. "She could be *your* munchkin. Have you thought about being a father? And please don't make a joke. I'm asking a serious question."

He thought it over while the plane slid through the clouds, the white puffs dragging along the windscreen. He needed to offer up honest answers if he wanted her honesty in return.

"I'm known as the commitment-phobic sort, so I guess the answer naturally follows that I never expected to be a father." He shrugged, eyes darting to the equipment on the dash. Everything was as it should be. "I'm careful," he added, hoping the comment reminded her just how attentive he could be.

She inched down the zipper on her parka, the sound hinting at the intimacies he wanted to share with her.

"Broderick? Do you like children?" Her question corralled his heated thoughts.

"I'm not sure I'll be a good father, but yes, I like children. I thought—hoped—I would be an uncle several times over by now." Like him, his siblings were focused on their careers and less focused on child rearing.

"I just wondered, because you've made a concerted effort not to hold her, even though I could swear I see the hint of a natural."

He thought about her words and the squeeze to his heart each time he saw the kid. "Oldest brother syndrome, I guess. I helped out with my siblings. But I honestly don't have much experience with babies beyond the occasional employee bringing in a new son or daughter to show off around the office."

"I hear Steele Oil has a top-notch on-site child care facility. I would assume you've seen it."

He nodded in her direction, keeping his eyes on the horizon. "Yes, I tour every part of the building."

"Hmm. So, the magazine photo shoot of you on the floor in the child care facility playing with toddlers wasn't a publicity stunt."

He could hear the playful smirk in her voice.

"You set me up with that lead in about the on-site day care."

"I did. Although I am curious. Was it a ploy to win women?" she asked with a challenge in her voice.

"I was there visiting a friend's child. I didn't know the photos had even been taken until they showed up in the article."

"That's nice to know."

"Don't let those photos fool you, though. I'm still not the go-to guy on anything more than the fractions for mixing formula. I'm hoping you know more than I do about what we're supposed to do with her."

They'd been dropped into caretaking with no warning. If Fleur was his, he would read all the books, figure it out.

"I have taken care of friends' babies," she said. "I have the nurse practitioner on speed dial, and we can look up answers on our phones. I expect you to give one hundred percent."

"Totally on board with that. Willing to learn what I don't know." He'd always been willing to solve tough problems. He just needed the chance to get acclimated.

"Which brings me back to my original question. What happens if she's your daughter?"

"Then I will be a father and I will work to be the best father I can be."

And he meant it.

Although with each moment that passed, he saw Glenna growing more attached to the baby. He couldn't help but worry about what it would mean for her to have no claim to the child.

His hopes of conversation making things easier between them had only reminded him of all the reasons this wasn't a simple getaway meant to end with them in bed.

Broderick was certainly full of surprises. Or perhaps, more accurately, she was seeing a version of him that she'd forgotten about.

His commitment to the potential of being Fleur's father reminded her of a twentysomething Broderick.

Memories floated in her mind's eye as she watched

him check some equipment, his lips forming a satisfied curl as he read the numbers.

In college, it had been Broderick's confidence that attracted her. They'd been assigned a group project— a task she normally dreaded. But he'd proved to be just as dedicated to the presentation as she was. He'd pulled all-nighters with her and they'd been excellent study partners, pushing each other to be better, smarter.

His gaze had always been electric and his body delicious.

It was still delicious. When he'd hefted the suitcase and supplies into the seaplane, he'd proved his muscles were just as tight and enticing as they had been over a decade ago. In that moment, the careful way she'd forced herself to think of Broderick as a cutthroat businessman faltered.

Chewing the inside of her cheek, she realized how much more there was to him and how damn difficult it'd be to spend all this time alone with him.

He was a *man*. In every sense of the word.

She tore her eyes off him now, searching for some distraction. She looked up into the mirror, half hoping Fleur would be waking and need her. But the infant slept on.

The plane dipped, hitting harder pockets of air as they made their way to the mountains.

Glenna devoured the sight of springtime in Alaska, particularly from the sky. A field of impossible emerald green and pockets of lakes served as contrast to the snowy mountains. When Glenna was a child, she'd thought of the land as a magical space. When she'd gaze out at the backdrop of green land and white mountains, it'd always seemed as if two seasons existed simultaneously.

She reached out to touch the cool glass at her side. The engine rumbled, reverberating slightly. "It's been so long since I flew in one of these."

"Perhaps because your family spent more time operating out of the Dakotas. I'm sure there are equally awesome sights you could show me there that I've missed."

"Sure, sure," she said, enticed by the idea of showing this man her stomping grounds. She folded her legs under her, sitting in the lotus position. "One good thing will come from this family merger. We'll bring new experiences to the table."

"I imagine there can be some other positives."

Did he have a hidden meaning in those words? His face appeared honest, calm, focused on flying. Lord, but he was handsome. The sun streamed through the window, playing across the strong line of his jaw, his broad shoulders in that plaid shirt, those jeans fitting him like denim was made just to hug that fine butt.

Her eyes roamed back up to the hard angles of his face. He always had that five o'clock shadow, even when he wore a crisp suit.

The man freaking oozed testosterone.

And her body sensed every pheromone.

She pulled on her black cashmere sweater, hoping the ritual tug on the sleeves would calm her. Ground her.

Staying in that cabin with him was going to be… difficult. To say the least.

She pulled her attention back to work and the more manageable reason for their retreat to the mountains. "Figuring out the corporate logistics of blending both employee rosters will be challenging," she reminded him, simultaneously reminding herself that Broderick Steele should be off-limits to her wandering feminine imagination. "There's no way everyone can keep their jobs at the current level. Demotions are inevitable. Everything can't be a co-job. Someone has to be the boss. CEO…CFO…" She ticked the list off on her fingers.

There. That should put some distance between them.

"We'll work it out," he answered vaguely, his hands clenching briefly on the steering yoke.

Strong hands. She remembered how they felt on her last night, his palm steadying her, burning through the fabric of her shirt.

"This peace between us can't last." She looked away from him, fingers tapping on her denim-clad thigh.

And no, she wasn't thinking about Broderick's touch on her thigh. It must be the cashmere sweater that was overheating her to this degree.

"Why not? Isn't there anything else in the company you would enjoy overseeing?" His question was a welcome distraction.

Did he really think she would give up her job without a blink? "Why should I be the one to find a new place in the business? What about you? Isn't there something else you would 'enjoy overseeing'?"

"In the end, it may not be up to either of us. Let's not make this getaway more difficult by arguing."

She studied him. No question, he had on his poker face today. She'd seen it often enough across the boardroom or on an occasional television show as he made a comment on behalf of his business. He was charming, sure, but gave little away.

Glenna played with the zipper on the folded parka in her lap, finding the interior of the small plane still too warm. "You're not going to attempt to push me out or seduce me into stepping aside?"

"Is that what you think I'm trying to accomplish here? Seducing you for Machiavellian gains?" His voice was dry as he adjusted their course.

"Aren't you?" There. She'd said it. Put it out there. Her heart picked up speed as she wondered what he would say.

And wondered even more what she *wanted* him to say.

His eyebrows shot up. "Well, in the past couple of days I've realized you're more plainspoken than I remembered. I'll answer as plainly as I can. I'm attracted to you and that has nothing to do with business. I always have been. Is that so difficult for you to believe? You're the one who walked out on our relationship. Not me."

Relationship. The word hit her hard. In fact, she never would have anticipated he'd characterize their time together that way. "It was a weekend."

He didn't back down. "It was a friendship that led to a weekend."

"A friendship? Are you sure? We barely knew each other. We thought we were Romeo and Juliet, rebelling against our parents."

"You were using me to get back at your parents?"

She stared hard out the window as they descended toward a lakeside cabin. Where they would be together. The flight had passed all too quickly.

Kota whined from the back, and Glenna's eyes flicked to baby Fleur. Still sleeping.

Broderick's question still hung in the air.

Looking intently at the cabin, noting the large fenced-in area and kidney-shaped hot tub, she spoke. "Isn't that what it was about for you?"

"Not at the time. No."

His words stole the air from her lungs and her stomach lurched as if the plane had just taken a significant plunge. "Then I'm sorry."

"But knowing that wouldn't have changed your leaving."

Would it have? She wasn't sure. It had been so long ago. And in the intervening years, she had met and loved her husband. His betrayal had shredded her heart. His death had nearly finished the job.

And now all the changes to their lives that had come so quickly? She couldn't afford the emotional stakes of another relationship.

"Our parents may have found a way to be a couple, but I can't envision that sort of strange, statistical improbability happening again in our family."

"Then it sounds like we have a challenge in front of us. Take care of the baby, who loves to sleep. Work on financials, which we can't start until tomorrow, when the latest reports come in. And work on becoming friends again, because, lady, we're stuck with each other."

After securing the plane, Broderick fixed his eyes on the mountainside cabin where Glenna and Fleur waited. That A-frame building held a lot of memories of family retreats for him.

The place had been one of his father's earlier acquisitions, when the stresses of work had started to take a toll on family time. Jack Steele had always told them family came first or the rest would fall apart. They'd been tight-knit, no question, and that had made it all the tougher after his mother's and sister's deaths.

He pulled gear out of the plane, one bag at a time, remembering so many other trips. Each kid had been responsible for packing his or her own duffel bag, and if they forgot a crucial piece of snow gear, that meant limited activities for that person. Jack made them learn their lessons the old-school way.

But they sure didn't forget a second time. Or in other cases, they learned to share and work together. Corporate team building, even back then.

Broderick's cell phone rang and he fished deep in his parka pocket. Reception up this way used to be tricky until his dad added a booster tower. Money sure did have its perks.

Broderick read the screen, but didn't recognize the number. Still, given the unknown situation with Fleur and the merger mess, he figured he'd better take the call.

"Yes, Broderick Steele speaking. And this is?" He hitched a carry-on bag and a large duffel with a portable crib over his shoulder, tucked the phone under his chin and then grabbed two more suitcases. Damn, babies came with a lot of stuff.

"Steele, this is Trystan Mikkelson," a gruff voice barked.

Glenna's brother, the one who worked their family ranch. The voice sounded familiar now that he'd identified himself. What did the guy want? "Is there a problem?"

"I'm checking on my sister."

Oh-kay. Broderick started his hike up the dock toward the cabin. "We arrived at the retreat on schedule. We're unpacking now and setting things up for the baby. Any news?"

"Nothing to report."

He frowned at the oddness of this call coming out of the blue from a man he barely knew. "Then please pass along the message to the rest of the family that we're fine. I'll send out periodic texts and emails with our progress on the business front. We would appreciate you sharing any news you receive."

There. That should appease his father that he was trying to make nice with the enemy—aka, his future stepsiblings.

"Can do," Trystan answered, his tone clipped. "And Steele? One last thing."

Broderick started up the steps, his eyes locked on Glenna. She stood at the floor-to-towering-ceiling window wall. "What would that be?"

"Hurt my sister and I will kick your ass clear to Canada."

The phone line disconnected.

Broderick dropped a suitcase and caught the cell as it slipped from under his chin. He studied the screen and saw the connection was fine, plenty of signal. Trystan had hung up on him. Plain and simple.

But the message had been clear enough, and oddly, for once, Broderick found himself commiserating with a Mikkelson. As a man. As a brother. Because if anyone hurt one of his sisters, Broderick would hunt the bastard down and pummel him personally.

His gaze trekked right back to the window and the woman who tugged at him in a way no other ever had.

With all that was going on in their families, he would have to tread very, very carefully.

Seven

Needing to collect her thoughts, Glenna sat on her bed, while Kota patiently settled at the door, head cocked to the side.

All her clothes had been neatly unpacked, hung in the closet or tucked away in drawers. Throughout dinner, she'd been the one to take care of baby Fleur. Not that she minded, but it concerned her. If the child was not Gage's… If the child was indeed Broderick's, then his avoidance was worrisome.

Perhaps he needed more time. Or perhaps she'd found the one area in his life where he didn't have a skill set and bravado.

She walked out of her room and into the main living area, the scent of pine furniture and floors cleaned with lemony oil filling the air. Broderick sat on the couch, eyeing Fleur in the baby swing. He seemed wistful, eyes warm, but he made no move toward the child.

Kota made laps around the baby swing, tail wagging. Protective. Eventually the dog curled on the dark brown throw rug in front of the hearth. They looked like a still life from a family vacation promotion.

Glenna scooped up Fleur, looked intently at her little face, again hoping a distinct feature would manifest and hint at her father.

Instead, she met Fleur's fluttering eyes, felt a connection to the infant and her innocence. Baby cradled in her arms, Glenna walked to the bedroom and put her down for the night. After turning on the monitor, she returned to the living area, fully taking in Broderick for the first time since supper.

Dressed comfortably as he was in navy jogging pants and a long-sleeved gray T-shirt, his muscles were on display. His dark hair slightly askew, he looked up at her.

The baby monitor hummed in her hand, giving her a sense of peace.

He jabbed a thumb in the direction of the French doors leading out to the deck. "I'm going to the hot tub. And that isn't a come-on line."

Hot tub?

Her body tingled with awareness at the suggestion. She tossed her hair over her shoulder with a nonchalant air she was far from feeling. "Glad to know you're not hitting on me, because if that's the best game you've got, you need help."

A masculine, throaty laugh rolled free. "I'll save my good game for later." He winked. "For tonight, after the stress of our parents' engagement and a surprise baby bundle, I could use some relief. I'm hoping to catch the northern lights. I never grow tired of seeing them stream across the sky and we're almost out of season. If you wish to join me, there are always extra swimsuits of all sizes in the changing rooms."

She studied him, wondering, assessing, and realized… "That's a dare, isn't it? To test your non-come-on line?"

"I'm simply stating where I'm going and inviting you to join me." He winked again. "If you dare."

How much did she trust him? Hell, how much did she trust herself?

But then ignoring him sure hadn't worked out all that well for her, given how much he occupied her dreams at night. "Fair enough. I'll bring the nursery monitor and join you once I choose the most boring swimsuit in the collection."

"I can't wait." His chuckle rumbled over his shoulder and hung in the air long after he stepped outside.

Once in the changing room, she thumbed through the neat stacks, her fingers lingering on an array of swimsuits stockpiled in the drawer until… There. She found it. The perfect boring suit in her exact size: a solid navy blue one-piece. Nothing would set the "hands off" tone quite like that. But a rush of impulse made her reach back into the drawer to a skimpy black string bikini.

She slid out of her clothes and into the bikini, then stared at her reflection in the mirror. Feeling confident and ready. Removing the hair tie from her wrist, she piled her strawberry-blond hair on top of her head—ready.

Before she lost her nerve, she shrugged into a luxurious spa robe and yanked fluffy boots onto her feet. She wasn't exactly a showstopper right now, but she couldn't deny she looked forward to knocking Broderick's socks off once her robe hit the deck.

Kota followed at her heels as she made her way to Fleur's room for a final check on her way out. The young pup wagged his fluffy tail in anticipation.

Kota bounded to the crib, his icy blue eyes curious and interested. While the dog meant well, he was too young to be left alone with Fleur. Glenna could too easily envision Kota jumping into the crib to curl around the baby. A well-intended action, but not one she could risk. Satisfied that Fleur was peacefully sleeping, she checked the monitor's setting once again before picking up her receiver, then guided Kota into the laundry room.

"Come along, boy. With me. With me," she commanded. She'd set up his crate, with a doggy bed so it felt like and smelled of home. Beside it, his bowl of water and a bowl of kibble waited. She'd even left some treats.

He pranced right to his bed and curled up with a sleepy sigh.

She smoothed the black-and-white fur along his side. "I love you, sweet boy. I do." She'd made sure to take him on extra long walks so he wouldn't get jealous of the attention she had to give Fleur. "You're a good pup. I'll see you soon. Night-night."

Standing, she turned on an iPod she'd rigged in the room to play soft, soothing music, the same she played for him at home. Then she dimmed the light and secured the gate in front of the door.

Turning on her heel, Glenna strode through the rustic cabin, her fluffy boots making muffled sounds on the stone floor in the kitchen. She made her way to the glass door that led to the picturesque deck extending out around the isolated cabin.

A watercolor sunset of reds and oranges melted over the snowcapped mountaintop, while to the east the evening's first stars appeared in the sky. She glanced about, taking in the serenity of the water, the slow bobbing of the parked seaplane. She followed the sound of churning water, walking past a latticework partition to the hot tub, which provided an uninterrupted view of the mountains.

And an equally chiseled Broderick.

The cold air urged her to move, but so did his whiskey-eyed stare. After stepping onto the heated stairs, she kicked off her fluffy boots, deciding somehow she could resist him better if she quickly slid into the warm, welcoming depths.

Although right now she was having trouble remembering why she needed to resist him at all.

Swallowing hard, she discarded her robe and

draped it over the railing. Her breasts tightened at the chill.

Or perhaps at the sight of the Broderick's bare, broad shoulders and his muscular arms stretched out along the edge of the hot tub as he leaned back. His smoldering gaze met hers. Then stroked over her from her nose to her toes.

He lifted one dark eyebrow. "If that's the most boring swimsuit in the collection, then heaven help me if you'd picked something else."

His words eased the stress knotting inside her and she stepped into the welcoming waters.

She sat next to him, careful not to get too close, not yet, not trusting herself. Leaning back, she rested her head on the edge, eyes fluttering shut at the caress of the jets easing her tensed muscles. "I'm sure there must be something in the code of ethics about a business meeting like this."

"Who says it has to be about business? We've crunched numbers, taken care of the baby..." His voice rumbled gently in the night air, soothing and intoxicating. "And we've helped our families. I say it's fine for us to decompress. I would have brought wine, but I want us both to be completely aware and in control of our senses."

She opened her eyes to find him staring at her, a hungry smile on his face. Her throat dried up as an answering hunger churned inside her.

One she tamped down with both fists clenched in the water. "Would you care to clarify that?"

"I want us sober for the baby, and in case I need

to fly the plane, of course. What did you think I meant?" he asked, with such overplayed innocence, she splashed him.

He splashed her right back, and then they both eased deeper into the swirling water, their legs brushing ever so briefly.

Emotional distance. She needed to keep finding some.

"Do you really think my mother and your father are going to get married?"

"What do you think?"

She shrugged, playing her fingers along the top of the water, popping bubbles. "My mother has dated a couple of times since my father died, but no one serious. For her to say she's marrying Jack is huge. I don't know your father well, only from business meetings and what I've heard."

"What do you think of him?" The timbre of Broderick's voice issued a bit of a challenge.

"He's fearless in the boardroom. His devotion to his family has always been without question."

"He loved my mother, deeply." Broderick held up a hand. "Sure, I know there are kids who wear rose-colored glasses where their parents are concerned. But he grieved so hard when we lost her and my sister. I don't believe the company would have survived if Uncle Conrad hadn't stepped in for a year."

"Somehow I never knew your uncle did that. He always seemed to have his own side projects going, independent of your father."

Broderick swirled the water and she felt the small

current against her tummy. "The family kept it on the down low to protect the stability of stocks. Uncle Conrad was masterful at reassuring the board. He comes across as such a jokester, but don't underestimate him. He's a smart man who doesn't care about recognition."

Stars twinkled in crystal brightness across the inky sky.

"Lack of ego in a man." She laughed softly. "What a novelty."

"Ouch." Broderick flicked water at her. "Surely you didn't mean that for humble me."

"Of course not." She crinkled her nose at him, feeling her body drawn toward his. Just like she had been over a decade ago. The laughter between them felt natural, familiar.

And so very enticing.

His hand lifted from the water to point to the beginning of the northern lights. Preternatural greens and purples filled the sky, dancing with no regard for anything besides the present moment.

Somehow, she and Broderick were closer than just a moment ago. She felt his body next to hers, aware and awake. Present.

Her eyes found his. Her own heart felt foreign in her chest, beating hard under his gaze. She wasn't sure who moved first, or if they perhaps moved at the same time.

Because without question, they were now a breath away from a kiss—a kiss of passion and longing and a promise of so much more.

And she didn't have the least inclination to stop.

* * *

So much for all his good intentions.

When she looked at him like that, he couldn't keep his distance. When her shoulder brushed against him, she released the desire he'd tamped down for a decade.

Her mouth parted, ever so slightly, anticipation pulsing in the small gesture. Broderick was filled with the urge to wrap his arm around her. Pull her onto his lap. To let her legs straddle him, for her to open to him, accept him as he plunged deep inside her body as he once had. As he wanted to do again.

This woman had always had the power to bring him to his knees with desire. And yes, the thought of being on his knees in front of her, with her legs parted, ready for him to tease her to completion—

He exhaled long and slow, willing his heartbeat to slow from a gallop to something vaguely close to normal.

The last time he'd surrendered to that temptation, she'd walked away, married another man and ignored him for a decade. Did he have the will to stop if he let himself have a taste of her?

Broderick stroked Glenna's cheek and plucked at a damp lock of hair clinging to moist skin. The silky softness of her sent a bolt of heat through him far hotter than the bubbling tub. Her pale blue eyes glistened with the reflection of the stars and hints of the northern lights.

Her creamy shoulders peeked above the rolling waters. The thin black ties reminded him she still wore a bikini top, and with one tug he could free those ties, baring her beautiful breasts for his eyes alone. He recalled in vivid detail what she looked like wearing nothing.

Yet there were more mature curves to her now and he ached to explore every inch with his hands and his mouth. To make love to her under the stars with the northern lights streaming through the sky.

He wanted that.

But if he didn't want another decade of regrets, he needed to bide his time. Take things slow.

For tonight, he needed to relearn the feel and taste of her lips.

Angling forward, he waited a hairbreadth away, giving her the chance to protest. Praying she wouldn't.

Then she slid closer. All the encouragement he needed to taste her, and for an instant he let himself do that. He brushed his mouth along her cheek, where his fingers had stroked only an instant before. Her skin was creamy soft. Her light gasp enticing as she swayed closer, her knees brushing his underwater.

Her breasts pressed against his chest with a sweet pressure that had him throbbing, longing to sweep aside her swimsuit and his and be inside her. The ache was intense, but the will to win her over for more than an impulsive hookup was stronger.

His mouth skimmed around to capture hers and her arms slid around his neck in a smooth affirmation that she wanted him as much as he wanted her. Heat and desire and the fragrant blend of Glenna mixed with the Alaska air threatened to send him over the edge of reason. Of control.

And in that moment, he realized just how very much he longed to be in her bed again. And again.

That second *again* being the operative word. If he moved too fast now, this could well be his only time with her. And once would definitely not be enough. He'd learned that long ago from a weekend that had tormented him for over a decade. He needed to be smarter this time.

With more than a little regret, he eased away, stroking his hands along her shoulders. "Glenna, continuing is not a smart idea."

"So you keep saying." Her breath caressed his face. Her own voice was ragged as she looked at him through her lashes. "You know how much I want you."

"Is that a proposition?" He stared deep into her eyes, a moment too long—just in time to feel more awareness pass between them.

"I'll let you know." She leaned in so close her lips feathered against his ear.

"Glenna, as much as I would like to continue this, it's too soon for both of us." He allowed himself one final stroke of her shoulders and a kiss on the tip of her damp nose. "Good night."

Easing away from her was no easy task, but he knew the time wasn't right. Not yet. With an extra dose of that regret charging through him, Broderick hefted himself from the water. And hell, yes, he welcomed that bracing cold wind whipping across the bay.

* * *

Jeannie Mikkelson didn't doubt her course. She'd been a businesswoman and a mother long enough to know her mind.

But she still found herself reeling from the impact of her feelings for Jack. A man she'd known for decades, only to suddenly find herself falling head over heels, passionately in love with him. How strange to fall for someone at first sight even when you already knew him. But that's what it had felt like. Seeing him with fresh eyes that day at the conference.

Now, stretched out on a leather sofa with him in his bedroom suite, the fireplace crackling, she was a part of his life, just as he was a part of hers. Not just dating or sex. Their daily routines were blending now that their romance was out in the open.

She looked at the remains of the simple dinner they'd shared, the tray on the coffee table. She knew well not to take the simple pleasures of life for granted.

If only others could understand that. "How can our children have so much in common and still be ready to knife each other in the nearest dark alley?"

His dry chuckle rumbled against her. "Might have something to do with the Hatfields and McCoys upbringing we gave them."

"You and Mary bad-mouthed the Mikkelsons?" She glanced at him, tracing his bristly mustache. Gracious, he was handsome, in a tall, dark and weathered way that launched flurries in her stomach. "I'm astounded."

Laughing, he nipped her finger. "Not Mary, but

I may well have shouted my frustration at the Mikkelsons over dinner."

"Why does that not surprise me?" She settled against his side, his arms warm and solid around her. "I guess we're reaping what we've sown."

"There's truth in that, I believe, but I also feel they're adults living their lives and we should be able to live ours."

Jeannie admired Jack's steadfast spirit, but wondered if they were being too rigid in their approach. "I don't mind being accommodating and reaching out."

"They're not babies to be coddled anymore. And this is about the business, as well. They can get on board or not."

There was no mistaking the steel resolve in his voice. He was aptly named.

"Jack, we can compromise with them."

"Bargain from a position of weakness?"

She turned to face him, resting her palms on his broad, flannel-covered chest. "We're talking about our family. That's much more important than the business."

"Once the kids realize that, they'll be fine." He clasped her hands and kissed the top of each. "But until then, someone's always going to feel they got out maneuvered by a new stepsibling. And we can't negotiate that. They need to figure it out on their own."

She could see his point. If only she could be sure he was right. "I just wish I knew your children better so I could gauge the dynamics."

He shifted his mouth to kiss her ring finger. "We need to go shopping for an engagement ring."

"I just want a band."

His mustache tickled her skin as he smiled. "Your feelings are heard, and I want to buy you an engagement ring."

Lord, he was stubborn. So was she. "Can you donate the money to charity instead?"

"I can do both."

Shaking her head, she eased her hands free and cupped his face. "You're a tough negotiator, Jack Steele."

"You keep me on my toes and I like that." He rested his forehead against hers, then angled his face to kiss her lips.

She welcomed him, thoroughly, opening and tasting.

Yet even as she lost herself in the moment, she couldn't stop her mind from spinning. She loved him, deeply. She would live the rest of her days with him. But she would never have children with him. All of that took some adjusting in her mind, given she'd expected to spend her life with Charles, the father of her kids. Things had upended for her when he'd died, and there were days she'd been certain her heart had broken so fully her body would follow. But somehow, she'd pieced herself back together.

For her children.

She'd held on for them. And now she couldn't deny a feeling of resentment that they were holding back. She'd always supported them in their decisions. Could they really cut themselves out of her life over this? Could she live with that?

Could Jack?

He'd truly lost a child, in the worst way imaginable. He had to be aching inside over this new rift. If it came down to calling off the wedding to keep their kids, even if *she* could commit, could she ask him to give up that much for her?

Eight

What. The. Hell.

Even fifteen minutes after Broderick left, Glenna was still stunned to her curling toes from his kiss—and his abrupt departure. She slumped against the side of the hot tub, the water bubbling just under her chin.

Broderick had literally walked away. After luring her out here under the stars. Kissing her as sweetly as if he was savoring the world's finest wine. Touching her as if she were delicate china to be adored. He'd then left her feeling more than a little crazy. Breathless and edgy, she could barely tell what side was up right now.

Leaning her head back, she stared up at the shimmering streaks of the aurora borealis. Early spring wasn't the optimum time to watch, but the lights were still magnificent. Romantic. She wasn't sure what game he was playing, or if it was even a game. He was attracted to her. He had high stakes here, too. Could he be as confused as she felt?

Asking seemed to be a dangerous proposition right now, though. Not until she was prepared for whatever his answer might be.

A wail interrupted her thoughts, sending her limbs into motion. Little Fleur's cry set off a maternal drive in her heart, and she barely registered the cold whip of Alaskan night air across her exposed skin as she leaped out of the tub and reached for the baby monitor. More discontented cries sounded from the machine.

Fumbling for her robe, she pulled it on as she made her way across the patio, dripping water as she went. She left her fluffy boots behind, determined to be there for the baby who might be her only physical link to her deceased husband.

Glenna yanked the door open, water pooling at her feet in the momentary pause. Entering the cabin, she heard another voice emerge as a rustle from the baby's room. A male voice.

Broderick.

On her tiptoes, she listened, trying to distinguish the words.

His tone, gentle and soft, made it hard to determine exactly what he was saying. Glenna touched a hand to her throat, held her breath.

Silence.

Little Fleur's crying eased.

Glenna scooped up a towel off one of the chairs at the rustic wood table. Patting herself dry, she strained to hear him, noting the warm shadows the yellow lamps cast in the cottage. A homey glow. There was no other way to describe this space.

"Shh, shh. It's okay, little one." His normally deep rasp carried a softer cadence.

Her head cocked to the side as she let him take care of the child. If Fleur was his baby, then this moment mattered for their bond. She didn't want to intrude on that.

Instead, she wandered around the cabin, reaching up to touch the moose antlers above the hearth. All the charm of old Alaska seemed distilled in this space. Glenna dropped her hand to the wood-burning stove. The metal was cool to her touch. An absence of fire. Refreshing, because her own conflicted desire felt like a roaring inferno.

"Ahh. There we go."

Broderick's voice sliced into her thoughts.

She kept moving around the room, her bare toes trading cool stone tile for a warm fur throw rug that sprawled in front of the couch.

Gazing about her, she took in the small details of the place. An old barn-style wooden sliding door separated the two rooms. As she drew closer, her breathing quieter now, she fully appreciated the softer side of Broderick.

Hand braced outside the door, she listened in on his one-sided conversation. Apparently, he'd picked up the baby, and she heard him say, "Yes, ma'am, we'll get you in a dry diaper and take a little walk around to look out the window…"

Her chest went tight as she envisioned him holding Fleur, carrying her to the window to gaze at the stars.

Glancing over her shoulder, Glenna noticed a family photograph hanging on the far wall, beneath massive elk antlers. The whole Steele clan… Crossing the room, she scrutinized it, aware of how different Broderick's family looked now. Aware of how strange it must be to go through life without his mother, without his younger sister who'd tragically passed away…

Fleur cooed, a gentle sound interrupting Glenna's melancholy thoughts.

A smile pushed at her lips and her heart beat a bit too fast. Glenna felt herself slip into dangerous territory, practically tap-dancing on thin ice.

Broderick's interaction with the child warmed her core.

Dangerous territory indeed.

A few hours had passed since he'd settled Fleur back to sleep. His potential daughter. The thought still sent him reeling.

He opened the door to the fridge, cool air dancing on his cheeks. Pulling at his soft navy T-shirt, he scanned the shelves for enticing treats for a late night work session. He had made progress with Glenna. He was playing a long game here. More than a one-night stand, and that required patience and persuasion.

Bold had always been his signature move, even

as far back as that weekend in college. Broderick didn't back down from challenges. And he needed her in his bed.

He would keep his cool, take his time and appeal to her more logical side. There was only one way to resolve this issue with the baby and with the business.

He needed to persuade her to make this about more than sex. They needed a serious relationship.

Then, problem solved with the business and the baby. They would be aligned on everything. He had no plans of marrying or falling in love, and she'd made it clear her dead husband was the love of her life. The notion of dating her, of taking it to the next level, should have surprised him, but it didn't. It settled in place like a well-formed plan for a profitable merger.

Reaching into the stainless steel refrigerator, he pulled out an assortment of cheeses—brie, feta and mascarpone. He stacked the wedges on the counter, then rummaged for the raspberries, blueberries, strawberries and smoked salmon.

He looked over his shoulder to where Glenna sat in the overstuffed chair, computer screen washing her face in a blue light. Her damp hair was gathered back in a lazy topknot that called to his fingers to pull it free.

After their hot tub dip, she'd pulled on silky sleep pants and a matching top. Sure, it covered her, but the outfit reminded him they were here for the night. The sea foam color brought out different hues in her blue eyes, like waters churned by a storm.

He understood the feeling well. But soon enough, they would have relief from this frustration—long-term relief—if he simply presented his plan in the right manner.

Arranging the bounty next to a sliced baguette on a cutting board, he felt resolved. Broderick would play his hand carefully. Walking away from her in the hot tub had been damn hard, but it had given him time to think. Time to come up with a better plan.

After bringing over the platter, he snaked two wineglasses between his fingers and grabbed a bottle of chilled prosecco.

He arranged the spread on the rustic dinner table, poured the sparkling wine and popped some strawberries into the stemmed glasses. Setting one to his right, he opened his laptop, ready to get down to business.

Looking up from her perch on the armchair, Glenna glanced at the food. She picked up her computer and briefcase, then headed for the chair next to his. The light scent of her cologne and shampoo wafted by him as she took her seat, so intoxicating his mouth watered.

After scooping smoked salmon onto a piece of bread, she studied him, her gaze so intense Broderick felt she could peer into his mind. There were a few moments of silence between them, interrupted only by the soft classical cello piece pouring through the nursery monitor, music for baby Fleur.

Kota groaned, extracting himself from his spot underneath the table to nuzzle Glenna's hand. Out of the corner of his eye, he watched her ruffle the pup's ears. Kota let out a large yawn, teeth flashing bright even in the muted light.

Broderick took a sip of his wine, peering over his computer screen. "We should talk about what happened out there."

A flush brightened her cheeks. "Let's not."

He squinted, taking in her forward-leaning posture. He wasn't buying for a moment that this attraction between them had simply been extinguished. She circled the rim of her wineglass with an idle finger, staring back at him.

In a throaty voice, he pressed on. "I want it to happen again, and more, and from your response it's clear I'm not alone in feeling the attraction."

He watched as she popped a raspberry into her mouth, the slight red stain of the juice accentuating her full lips with a sweetness he wanted to savor. Reminding him of the earlier kiss that still seared his brain and left him feeling more than a little uncomfortable.

She wasn't easily swayed. She shrugged her shoulders. "It's biology. And abstinence—" She winced. "I didn't mean to say that part about being abstinent. That's personal. Private. None of your business. Please don't speak right now."

The scarlet in her cheeks deepened.

After spreading goat cheese on a piece of baguette, he eased back in his chair and gave her his best, wickedest smile, teasing her just a little. Although the fact she hadn't been with anyone since her husband's death reminded Broderick of how much she'd cared for the other man.

He moved his neck from side to side to work out a sudden kink.

The knowledge also reminded him that he was on the right track with his plan for something more serious with her. She preferred sex within a relationship.

"Really, don't say a word." She buried her face in her hands, then fluffed her hair and returned to her wineglass. Glenna's next swig seemed full of determination.

Silently, he held up his hands.

She threw a pillow from the neighboring chair at him. "You know I'm attracted to you, but you made it clear in the hot tub that nothing is going to happen," she said boldly. "I don't know what your angle is, but I'm not into game playing. You've only served to remind me why it's unwise to act on those feelings, especially with all that's going on." She made a gesture that seemed to suggest she was talking about all the general chaos of their lives.

For him, that chaos wasn't insurmountable. If she wanted to opt for a no-holds-barred discussion, he could handle that. In fact, he welcomed the challenge of sparring with her.

"I walked away earlier because I wasn't sure you're ready. Am I right?"

Her eyes narrowed and she scratched under her topknot in a gesture he was beginning to realize was her nervous twitch. A poker "tell" that she was rattled.

"Maybe. But you could have said all of this out

there instead of just strutting away like the lord of the manor."

"I could have, but you tempt me, lady. In spite of my very best intentions, you tempt me."

"I guess that's a compliment." Her throat moved in a long swallow. "Things are difficult and complicated here. I'll admit that. It would help if you weren't so smart. So charming. So damn hot."

The way she spit out the words, they didn't sound much like compliments. Still, he grinned.

Broderick grabbed another handful of berries. "I'm glad you feel that way. Those should be good things, because you're one helluva sexy lady. I'm pacing myself. You're worth the wait." He finished his white wine and popped a berry in his mouth.

She pursed her lips, shaking her head. "That still doesn't answer the question of how we're going to work together and be in the same family."

He scooted his chair closer. "What if we work together, at the office, and take Fleur with us?"

"What do you mean?" Her brow furrowed. Glenna downed her last bit of wine, then licked her lips. Driving him mad.

He needed this to work.

"You don't want to get married again. You've said as much. I'm devoted to my job, but I want a steady relationship."

"Just not the commitment?"

He nodded. "I don't want my heart stomped by someone too upset by the hours I pull, and I sure as hell don't want to go through what my father went through when Mom died. So let's give this a try hanging out together. Seeing where the attraction takes us."

Broderick tucked a loose strand of hair behind her ear. Let his other hand graze her knee ever so slightly.

"You're serious? You're not just hitting on me for a one-time deal?" Glenna leaned into him, her voice soft.

"I'm very serious. Look at this as the most important business decision of our lives. We'll be together, connected. Then whoever turns out to be Fleur's new parent, we can help the other."

Her blue eyes searched his. "You really mean this."

"Can you think of a good reason why not? Let's decide now."

"Whoa. You're asking us to make this kind of decision right now, this fast." She held up her hands, shaking her head until that topknot slid to the side, threatening to fall altogether. "That's crazy."

"Maybe. Maybe not." He slid a berry between her lips. "Think on it."

Her throat moved in a long, slow swallow. Yes. He was making significant progress.

He eased back. "Now let's get to work on the last set of financial quarterlies."

Kota had limitless energy, or so it seemed to Glenna. For the past hour, she'd played fetch until her arm grew weary. Kota dashed into the snow, a sleek black line of ambition. Then he'd bound back to Glenna, practically prancing with the ball wedged between his teeth.

And maybe she'd been trying to work off the nervous energy from the chaos Broderick had brought to her life with his proposition.

She pitched the tennis ball again. Harder.

The midmorning sun hung heavy in a cloudless sky, and the cabin's isolation provided her with time to think. Much needed time to think, as it turned out.

Sure, she felt a visceral attraction to Broderick. But his proposition about starting a serious relationship and co-raising Fleur?

That she still had to work out. Her feelings ran rampant, and over breakfast, she'd snapped at him. Not on purpose, but she'd known she'd been prickly.

Too much had changed in a week. Nothing about her life felt normal or manageable. The only things that had become increasingly clear were her affection for Fleur—and her desire for Broderick. She knew she had to consider his offer.

She called Kota back to her, and they made their way from the fenced-in backyard to the deck and hot tub. Broderick opened the door, a concerned look on his face.

The echoes of hurt on his face slammed into her. "I'm sorry for being irritable earlier. Truce?"

"Absolutely." His smile rested easy on his tanned face. Those whiskey eyes warmed.

"Would you like to come with me while I walk Kota? I think Fleur could use some sunshine, too."

She gestured to the small nature path she'd spotted just outside the fence.

He gave a backward glance into the cabin, where Fleur sat in a baby carrier. "Won't she get sick from the cold?"

"Seriously? Were you Steele children pampered wimps?" Glenna laughed, welcoming a moment's levity.

"Don't let my dad hear you say that. He believed in making us work hard. No silver-spoon, trust-fund kids in his family." Broderick took a step back so she could make her way into the cabin. Even so, her body rubbed against his, sending electric awareness into her limbs.

Glenna ignored it, responding instead with a tidbit about her own life. "Mom and Dad were the same way. We even had price limits on eating out. I remember someone commenting on it at a restaurant. Mom said, 'Yes, Charles and I have a healthy portfolio. Our children, however, have yet to earn their fortune.'" Glenna did her best to impersonate Jeannie's dramatic hand waving.

Broderick let out a chuckle, nodding as if thinking of some distant memory. "Sounds like Dad... And if we're not careful, they're going to fire all of us and start with a fresh staff."

A deep, rich laugh emerged from her. Shook her back to life. "Okay, now let's get you ready for that walk."

"What do you mean?" He pointed to his coat, as

if that was all there were to their excursion. "I have my winter gear."

Raising a brow, she gestured to the carrying pack in the living room. "You'll need to keep Fleur close to your chest so she'll be warm and secure."

"What about a baby sled instead?" he asked quickly.

He was obviously nervous, but Glenna recalled how he'd handled Fleur last night when no one was looking. A natural. Though he clearly needed encouragement.

"This is a difficult time, with her being away from her mother. The baby needs as much human contact as we can give her."

"I could walk the dog." His counteroffer was smooth, but didn't completely mask his unease.

"Are you afraid of babies?"

"No. I'm afraid of that contraption." He walked to the swaddle pack, picked it up. He examined it gingerly, as if it might move of its own volition.

"Think of it as a hiking pack on your front."

She quickly assembled Fleur in the pack on Broderick's chest, showing him how it worked and barely resisting the temptation to take a little extra time touching him. Things were…complicated. This walk would do them good. If Fleur was his, he had to learn.

Glenna playfully squeezed his arm. "And now we're ready to walk."

She let him lead. After all, these were Steele family grounds. He'd grown up here, knew the trails. Kota walked in step with them, and Glenna drank in the untouched scenery. Not another building in sight. Perfection—she'd found it.

They hiked toward the mountain, boots crunching in the unmarked snow. Silence descended between them, the comfortable familiar kind. Fleur made giggling noises, soft and lovely. Broderick seemed to calm down the farther they went.

Feeling empowered and brave out in nature, Glenna asked, "Do you think our families would have been friends if they'd all worked for the same business or if we'd lived in the same neighborhood?"

"Hmm... That's an interesting thought. The Steeles and Mikkelsons going to block parties together."

Her lips felt slightly chapped by the persistent wind. "Silly question. I'm just feeling whimsical, I guess."

"It's not silly at all. I imagine we would have built forts and had snowball wars."

She chewed her lip before adding, "Boys against the girls, naturally."

"I bet you girls would have won. Especially with my sister Breanna on your side."

"That's the first time I've heard you mention her." The loss must have been monumental. She felt for him. She understood loss well.

"That seems wrong somehow, that I don't talk about her more. She should be remembered." His voice sounded honest and raw. She knew sharing this must be hard for him, but he'd said he wanted to be friends. He wanted more. Could she be there for him?

"Do you want to tell me something about her?" When her grandmother was alive, she'd often talked about people in her life who had already passed on. She'd tell stories of their lives, and in doing so, had preserved a part of them. That was a small gift Glenna could offer Broderick.

"She was full of spirit and one helluva leader in the making."

Glenna snorted. "Naomi is spirited."

He laughed and rolled his eyes. "Naomi is a rebel. Breanna was more focused, always charging forward, so I figured I better keep up. She made me stronger."

"Losing someone you love is so hard. There's no set way for how to deal with it. We're all different. Losing your mother at the same time is just horrible." All losses hurt. To death, to divorce, to time.

And therein lay the core of why this offer to start something serious with him gave her such pause. She needed to make him understand that committing to a relationship, even without being in love, wasn't something to be taken lightly, no matter how much it streamlined their practical concerns.

"We were all changed because of it." Broderick stopped walking for a moment to stare at her. "I'm so very sorry about your husband's death. This has to be hell for you, waiting for the paternity results."

She swallowed, pushing her feelings to the pit of her stomach. "I'm sure it's difficult for you, as well, not knowing if Fleur is yours."

"It's different for me. I understand that." He squeezed Glenna's hand.

"Are you trying to ask me if I really think she could be his?" She found it impossible to keep a neutral tone.

"There's no need for me to ask. The test will speak for itself." His evasive answer did nothing to soothe her.

"But you want to know if I believe my husband would cheat on me." That was the question he wasn't asking.

"It's not my place to ask. But I do care if he hurt you or betrayed your trust." Broderick looked at her.

She inhaled deeply, smelling the pine, letting the crisp air steady her. In a small voice, she answered him. Gave him a secret few people knew. "He had an affair three years ago. We worked through the problem with a counselor. It wasn't easy, but we put our marriage back together."

"Damn, I am so sorry." He turned to face her, concern etched in the lines on his brow and at the corners of his mouth.

"He's dead." She could barely choke out the words. "I'm sorry most of all about that."

"Of course," he said gently.

"I told him if he cheated again, that would be a deal breaker. But I can't help thinking that if he *had* cheated again, he wouldn't have risked telling me because he knew I would walk."

"And?" Broderick's head tilted.

"What do you mean? Isn't that enough?"

He stared intensely at her. "There's more on your face."

"If Fleur is his child…it means he betrayed me again. And yet I don't know how I can let go of her. She's the last piece of him. I know that sounds all tangled up—that I would have left him for being unfaithful, but thinking of her being his child makes me ache. We had trouble conceiving. I have endometriosis and lost an ovary during an ectopic pregnancy." She drew a deep breath. Then another. All the pain of the last few years rushed through her.

Broderick reached to stroke her hair.

She leaned into his touch for an instant before pulling away. "I don't want sympathy. I just want answers." She cleared her throat. "What are your plans if the test shows you're her biological father?"

He looked down at Fleur, whose eyes had shut. Her breath was deep as she slept. He smiled at the baby. "I'll be her father. She's already suffered enough rejection from her mother."

"One way or another, she will be staying with our new extended family."

"Appears so. You're good with her."

Glenna smiled as she moved closer to look at Fleur. "I love children. I've always wanted to be a mother."

"You can still be a mother, no matter the outcome of the DNA test."

There he went. Pushing that offer at her again. The one she had no idea what to do with. "I realize that, but I don't want to discuss it. Thank you for caring."

He touched her face. This time, she lingered, staring into those eyes. Lifting her head, she closed her own, and her lips found his…

Instantly, she was entranced by the warmth of his tongue, a brilliant contrast to the cold of the air. His hands found her hair, pulling her closer, becoming more urgent...

The world tilted. Literally.

Kota pounced on them, flattening Glenna to the ground. As she stood, dusting off her jacket, she couldn't help but think how the pup had saved her from herself.

Nine

Losing himself in memories of past winter meals at the cabin, Broderick flipped open the lid of the slow cooker. He checked the status of his family's recipe for caribou stew. A roll of steam billowed out with the scent of thyme. He waved some of the fog toward his face, breathing in the smell of the hearty meal promising a flavor he found only in Alaska. Comfort food, really.

His personal favorite, and he looked forward to sharing it with Glenna after she finished putting the baby to bed. At the moment, she was oblivious to his nostalgia, sitting on a quilt on the living room floor with Fleur and some activity toy.

His parents would sleep in the master bedroom. The girls slept in the small spare room—a room

Fleur would use now—and the boys would sprawl out in the loft. Family time was full of snowmobiling, fishing and hikes, until they came back to the cabin exhausted and famished, leaving a trail of soggy snowsuits, caps, gloves and boots behind them.

This recipe came down from his grandmother. Every time he made the stew, he envisioned his grandma and mother dicing the tomatoes and onions. They didn't need to measure the broth and spices. Everything was done by eye, and even when his family had become richer than Midas, with a crew to help in the home, his grandmother had insisted the recipe wasn't falling into any stranger's hands. And that even if a staff chef attempted to recreate the recipe, no one could cook the stew as well as she could. Broderick agreed.

The caribou stew recipe was a part of their family DNA.

Taking a wooden spoon off the ceramic spoon rest, he stirred the chunky soup, which had been simmering all afternoon, checking the color and consistency. He felt as if someone was staring at him and looked up to find Kota sitting pretty. Those icy blue eyes left no mistake. The puppy was working his charm for a treat.

"Kota, buddy, I'm not sure I'm supposed to feed you table scraps," Broderick said. "Glenna would probably kick my butt."

"Yes," she called out, "I will kick your butt if you mess with my pup's good manner."

The pup tilted his head and let out a whimper.

"Yeah, yeah, puppy," Broderick continued, half amused at her speedy response. "I know it's not fair. But I'll tell you what. I do have a soup bone tucked away in the fridge and if your mama says it's okay, you can have that all to yourself. Right, Glenna?"

"After I check to make sure the bone won't splinter or make him sick," she called back, tapping a jingling toy, enticing Fleur to reach for it.

Kota kept waiting expectantly, making Broderick feel like the meanest human alive. He checked that Glenna wasn't looking, and then pulled out a chunk of cooked meat and rinsed it.

Kneeling, he whispered to the puppy, "Our secret. You can have it if you work for it, okay? Your mama says the key to a balanced, well-trained dog is the motto 'Nothing in Life Is Free.' So here's the deal. You do one of your tricks and I'll give you this piece of meat. Fair enough? Now shake, Kota, shake," he commanded.

Kota lifted his paw on cue and Broderick felt as if he'd clinched a million-dollar deal. He shook the paw, then passed the nibblet to the dog on an open palm. The puppy took the treat with a gentle lick.

"Good boy, Kota." Broderick gave the husky a scratch behind the ears before standing, washing his hands and returning to his meal prep.

He scooped up a taste, assessing the balance of game and spices to make sure none overpowered the other. His taste buds all but moaned in pleasure. Sure, it could use a little tweaking, but the stew was almost perfect. Almost. He looked forward to sharing the meal with Glenna tonight as he stepped up his plans to persuade her they could be good together—

His cell phone chime cut through his thoughts.

Leaving the spoon half submerged in the contents of the slow cooker, he fished his phone out of his pocket as Kota trotted into the living area and sprawled out in front of the fireplace a good inch away from the baby's quilt, as Glenna had already taught the puppy. Glenna promptly pulled two all-natural doggy treats from her pocket to reward him.

Nothing in life was free.

Chuckling and impressed, Broderick looked back at his chiming phone. A picture of his brother Marshall popped up on the screen. Sliding his finger to answer, Broderick scanned the spice rack, looking for black pepper, to kick up the flavor a notch.

He held the phone to his ear, instinctively lowering the volume. A silly gesture, really. Glenna could hear his side of the conversation from her spot a few feet away.

Regardless, he stole a glance at her, taking in the tight-fitting dark-wash jeans and blousy aqua top that suggested the beauty of her curves. She wasn't paying attention to him, though. Instead, she'd scooped up Fleur and was cradling the baby in her arms with a smile.

"Hey, Marshall. Good to hear from you. Any news on tracking down the baby's mother? Or the father?"

That last question had his gut in knots, because he didn't have a clue which way he wanted this to shake down.

"No answer yet on either front, I'm sorry to say," Marshall said, the sound of a horse's whinny floating through the phone line. "She disappeared into Canada and not a peep since then."

Broderick ground more black pepper into the slow cooker, then stirred the stew as he watched Glenna coo to Fleur some nonsensical words that made him grin.

"Damn, who dumps their baby and just disappears? Doesn't check on the child? Nothing?" He turned around, eyes skating to baby Fleur.

Her round face beamed with happiness and light. All things good and innocent. Fleur grinned up at Glenna, whose face was obscured by strawberry-blond tendrils. A stranger peering in through the window at this moment would easily believe Glenna was the mother. Her attentiveness and empathy manifested in every movement.

Damn. This woman pierced him. Humbled him.

"I don't have the answer for that," Marshall said, always matter-of-fact.

"I realize Deborah didn't have any family to support her when she had the baby. But if Fleur is mine, why didn't Deborah reach out to me before?" Broderick felt sick at the idea that she would think he wouldn't have assisted her. Things might not have worked out between them, but there'd be no way in hell he'd let his child suffer because of that. Family over all else. And if Fleur was his, he intended to ensure that.

"Maybe she was worried about the family money and losing her child," Marshall offered.

"I wouldn't deprive a child of its mother. I would just want rights—" Defensiveness and anger weighed down his heart.

Marshall interrupted, "I know, brother, I know." A long sigh filled the earpiece. "But it's obvious she's not thinking clearly. And then perhaps she became overwhelmed? I'm just guessing."

Exhaling hard, wanting to accept that explanation, needing some reason for this, Broderick willed his frustration down a notch. He set aside the pepper mill and sampled the stew again. Hmm…almost but not quite. And as he tasted it once more, he couldn't help but wonder if he was substituting a fixation on food for his hunger for Glenna, trying to ignore the other appetite that threatened to burn him.

Patience. The key for winning the battle with Glenna *and* with conquering this recipe. He hoped if he kept at it, he'd match his mom's skill one day. Was it a small way of recapturing a bit of the people he'd lost? Maybe.

The stew still missed something. He stared blankly at the spice rack, phone pressed hard into his ear. "I guess we'll never know until she tells us. Hopefully sooner rather than later."

"No kidding." Marshall gave a low whistle. "Naomi is working hard to research all legal aspects so we're prepared, whatever we face."

"Glad to know, for Fleur's sake. Naomi's a fierce

advocate." Thankfully. He had a feeling they needed Naomi's ambition and ferocity.

Glenna had laid the baby on a blanket decorated with blue and pink polar bears. She patiently changed Fleur's diaper, making silly sounds as she went. Even from this distance he could see how comfortable the child was. The baby had two mighty advocates on her side with Glenna and Naomi. And he couldn't deny the protectiveness for the kid building in him. "I've wondered more than once why Dad doesn't put Naomi in charge of the company. She's a fighter."

He could practically see his brother shake his head, scratching under the brim of his Stetson. "You're telling me. Naomi actually asked Dad about a prenup for his marriage to Jeannie."

"Holy crap," Broderick said, then whistled softly. "Did he explode?" Naomi had never been shy by a longshot. Their father said she'd come out of the womb arguing, already a lawyer in the making. She always spoke her mind, even in difficult or touchy situations. His sister had a way of seeing the world through Lady Justice's eyes—objectively and full of reason.

"Not really, surprisingly. He said he understood those prenups were to protect the husband and the wife so their interfering children knew where things stood. And so we won't have to feel conflicted, he and Jeannie are using independent counsel to set up the will." On the other end of the phone, Broderick could hear more whinnying of horses. Perhaps Marshall was getting ready for a ride to clear his mind.

Broderick could only imagine how chaotic it must be at the family property right now.

"Okay, then. So we have no idea what's going on?" His eyes slid back to Glenna. She'd put the baby in pajamas. Scooping Fleur up, she cradled the child to her chest, completely unaware of Broderick's gaze.

Or the fact that he was remembering the perfection of her curves in that bikini she'd worn for their dip in the hot tub.

"Correct. He said it was none of our business. They are adults. And that we all have our own fortunes, so we don't need anything from them."

Broderick laughed, respecting the old man more than ever even when, sure, it would have been a lot easier to be in the loop. "Fair enough. Looking at the financials I've seen so far, the two companies are fairly evenly matched. I'm actually surprised. We've both been so damn busy trying to convince the other we had the edge, we didn't realize we were running neck and neck."

Even while he talked to his brother, Broderick's thoughts were on Glenna and how soon he could get her back into the hot tub. Or better yet, stretch her out on that bearskin rug and make love to her by firelight.

"We don't have to worry that Jeannie and her kids might try to take advantage of Dad for his money."

"And they don't have to worry we're trying to take advantage of their mom, since we're all standing soundly on our own fiscal feet."

Marshall's tone was indifferent. Broderick knew

something was weighing on his brother's mind. "That's worth a bit of peace, at least."

Broderick leaned back against the counter and watched Glenna rock the baby. Fleur burped, then giggled. "Remember Mom's friend, Christy Shackleford, who married Dad's doctor? Her two sons were hell-bent from day one that their mama wasn't getting enough of the old man's estate even though he'd made provisions for the rest of her life backward and forward."

"Yeah, I do," Marshall said drily. "They guilted their mama into sneaking them money under the table while the old man was alive, and then when he died, they took the rest."

Turning back to the stew, Broderick tasted it again. There. That was right. He closed the lid. "He'd left a rock-solid will, but those boys beat the hell out of things in the legal system. Whittled the estate down to next to nothing just getting them to back off, and the poor woman barely had anything left."

"Things can get touchy when two families come together so late in life," Marshall said pointedly. "And I don't have the past you and Glenna do. You're stuck up there together with the baby and that whole paternity issue hanging over your head. Watch out for yourself. Okay?"

Broderick bristled as he chose two deep pottery bowls from the cabinet. "Greed is a hungry beast. No matter how much you feed it, it still dies of starvation."

"Are you saying we should count our blessings?"

"That's one way to look at it." He pulled out a loaf of crusty sourdough bread and set it on the wooden carving board. With a ceramic knife, he sliced thick pieces. The perfect accompaniment to the stew.

Marshall paused before continuing, "What's your take on Glenna?"

"She's worried her job will go away," Broderick said without hesitation, settling on the most benign answer he could find, because he was not talking about the kiss or his hopes of renewing their relationship.

"Valid concern about the job, really."

It was premature to discuss who the CFO would be. He was still hoping she would choose a different job and remove the controversy altogether. "She wants her mother to be happy." There was plenty of drama to go around. "And she's attached to the child already. She's afraid of the kid getting lost in the system and she is not going to want to let that child go."

A pause stretched over the phone line before Marshall continued, "Even if the baby was the product of her husband cheating?"

"I believe so." And what did that mean for him? Broderick wanted Glenna, but was he prepared to use, really use, the baby to get her? He was a tough businessman, but the harshness of using a child for leverage gave him pause.

"If she already is so attached to this kid, what's going to happen if the baby turns out to be yours?"

Damn good question. He hoped she'd say yes to his proposition and make that question void. But no matter what occurred, their time together was only going to get more complicated once the answers about the baby came through.

Leaning back against the counter again, he watched Glenna stand, then her slender silhouette disappeared as she went into Fleur's room to put the baby down for the night.

Complicated didn't even begin to describe this scenario.

If he wanted to win Glenna back in his bed—and he did—he would have to step up his game.

Jack dived into his indoor pool, the warm waters enveloping him. He had never been much for team sports, other than watching his kids play. His life was already complicated enough, at home and at work. He enjoyed recreation that afforded him time alone or one-on-one moments with those important to him. Outdoors when possible, but he kept indoor options available for himself and wearing out his kids. Like with this pool and an indoor gym.

He gravitated toward activities like fishing, hunting, swimming and sledding. He'd tried teasing Glenna that he could turn Kota into a sled dog.

She hadn't laughed.

Stroking easily, he kicked toward the other end of the pool, where Jeannie lounged on the steps. The rippling water did little to mute the appeal of her body in a sleek black swimsuit. He got plenty of time alone with her these days as their kids kept their distance, communicating via email about progress on baby Fleur and the merger of the companies.

The child was about the only issue where they agreed.

His and Jeannie's efforts to smooth over the blended family transition weren't going as planned. And he could sense her frustration growing. More and more each day. If she asked him one more time if they should delay the wedding, he was going to blow a gasket.

A final kick underwater propelled him the rest of the way to Jeannie's side. He broke the surface next to her and turned to sit on the stone steps. The hot tub bubbled a waterfall into the main pool.

She skimmed her elegant arms along the surface, trailing her hands. Her ring finger was still bare, but they'd met with a jeweler to have one custom made. "Maybe we should delay the wedding."

Damn it.

He ground his teeth and held his temper in check, wishing some of the snowflakes on the glass ceiling could rain down on his heated feelings. "Jeannie, if we back down now, our stubborn children will just keep pushing. We taught them their negotiation skills. We shouldn't be surprised they're using them against us."

"What if this push and tug isn't a game?" She tucked a damp blond strand into her hair band, gathering her locks on top of her head. "What if they really mean it? What if one or more of them cuts off from the family?"

"You're borrowing trouble. They're blood. They're

not going anywhere." He refused to accept otherwise. This was the time in their lives where he and Jeannie should be handing over the reins and enjoying at least a partial retirement. He wanted her to enjoy these recreational moments and relax.

Except life kept getting tenser. He pressed his leg against hers.

"Jack, are you certain?" Her forehead furrowed and she inched away from him. Again. "Because I'm not."

"Yes, I'm sure of that." He reached for her hand, only to have her avoid his touch. "But I'm starting to wonder if there's something more going on here. Do *you* want to delay the wedding because *you* are having doubts?"

"Honestly?" She inhaled deeply, her hands clenching into fists. "I'm worried about you. You lost a child already. I don't want to be the cause of you losing another."

Her words chilled him as surely as if the ceiling had opened up to dump the snow on top of them.

"That's not the same, Jeannie, and not playing fair."

Her jaw thrust forward, stubbornness stamped all over her features. "You wanted to know what I'm thinking and there it is. I don't know if I can live with myself if I cause you to lose another child in any fashion."

"I call bull." He pointed, stabbing the water with his finger and letting flow the words he'd been bottling, the thoughts he'd been denying. "I think you're looking for an excuse to back out because things are getting tough and you're afraid of losing your kids. You're flinching at the clinch of the negotiation."

"This isn't a negotiation, Jack," she said, her voice rising with frustration. She shot to her feet, water dripping from her body as she stalked out of the pool. "This is our lives. Our children. Our hearts."

He followed her, fear filling his gut. He took her hand just as she reached for a fluffy towel. "You are my heart."

"It's not that simple." She turned to face him, their hands clasped between them.

"For me, it is just that simple."

She shook her head, backing away. "You're deluding yourself. Life is never as simple as 'love solves all.'"

Her words sank in, but more than the words, he saw her face. Felt her letting go, his whole world slipping out of his grasp. "You're breaking things off."

"I just… I need…" She gathered a towel to her chest and backed toward the changing room. "I'm going home, and no, I don't know when I'll be back. Jack, please honor that. We need space right now."

As he stood with water pooling around his feet, he could do nothing more than let her go. For now. His heart was broken, but he would not let that defeat him. He refused to believe he wouldn't have the chance to place an engagement ring—and wedding band—on her finger.

He would do whatever it took—when the time was

right—to convince that stubborn woman they were meant to spend the rest of their lives together.

Glenna had just settled Fleur down for the night. The day in the snow had been exhausting—and rewarding.

Quietly, she slid shut the barn-like door to the baby's room and made her way back to the living area where—

Her stomach flipped and her heart squeezed. She blinked, barely able to believe her eyes. But sure enough, a lovely, thoughtful gesture was laid out for her. A small dinner table had been pulled in front of the crackling fire. A romantic gesture—the kind born of simplicity and earnestness. This man could afford to hire legions of caterers. Writing a check was easy for someone like him—or her. She knew the effort that had gone into what he'd done for her.

Two bowls of stew with steam rising framed a plate of thickly sliced bread. The Steele family's personal beer label on a large longneck bottle glinted in the firelight. Two beer mugs were filled with the pale foaming brew.

A real home-cooked dinner. It'd been ages since she eaten something that wasn't ordered in or prepared by professional staff. Even when home, she avoided the kitchen. Cooking for one had been difficult, a glaring reminder that rendered her husband's death all the more palpable.

This gesture touched her heart on so many levels.

A candle flickered on the table, adding to the spicy aroma of the caribou stew. They both could buy whatever they wanted, which made the personal touch and effort mean more to her.

He draped a hand towel over his arm and smiled with that wicked glint in his brown eyes. "Dinner is served."

His attention was completely on her. A heady sensation. She felt the warmth of his gaze touch her skin, send her reeling. He looked so sexy, standing with the chair pulled out for her, his dark hair slightly messy.

"Thank you, Broderick. This is truly thoughtful of you." She took her seat, enjoyed the brush of his fingertips as he guided the chair forward.

"I realize you've been doing the bulk of baby care. It's only fair I pull my weight where I can. I'm definitely a better cook than I am a diaper changer," he joked, his laughter rumbling up to the vaulted ceiling.

The beauty of the fire was nothing compared with the magnetism of this man as she sat across from him. Needing to break the spell, she looked out the window, drank in the fading sun splashing the little valley in orange and red, recalling an artist's palette.

The scenery, too, failed to distract her, being just as romantic as this dinner. She might as well surrender to the moment.

She picked up her spoon, scooped up a bit of stew. Silence lingered between them as she tasted the first bite. The flavor rolled along her taste buds. Bliss. She'd had caribou stew before but nothing like this. She couldn't hold back a sigh of delight.

"Oh my, this is… I don't even have words to do it

justice. Such rich flavor. I could go on, but I'm too hungry." She spooned up another taste as he laughed.

His smile of appreciation sent a thrill tingling through her. Everything about this moment had her senses on high alert, like a conduit in a lightning storm.

Across from her, the fire whispered its approval, flames leaping like dancers in a perfectly coordinated ballet. A structured, beautiful dance. Much like the one she had to perform now, to keep this surprisingly thoughtful, yet devilish man from making her life more complicated.

They ate quietly, the food so delicious she realized how truly famished she was. Her finger brushed his when they both reached for a piece of bread. Glenna's cheeks flooded with heat, but she hoped the firelight disguised the betrayal of her feelings.

Zeroing in on the sight of the mountain and elk emblem on the Steele logo, she realized she felt strangely comfortable here. Glenna felt the weight of his gaze on her, and looked up.

He tipped his head to the side, his eyes narrowing quizzically. "What happened to you?"

Such a loaded question.

"Care to be more specific?" She took a slow sip of her beer, enjoying the hoppy flavor.

"You used to be so…open." He set aside his half-eaten piece of bread and leaned forward.

"You mean back when I was naive? Before I married a man who cheated on me?" The darkness in her tone came as a defense to the pain she'd experienced.

Broderick shook his head, eyes shifting to hers.

"No, I don't mean that. Not at all. In college, you were funny and you smiled. God, you smiled in a way that slayed me."

"I haven't lost my sense of humor. I smile, and I help others. Maybe you're the one who's changed," she volleyed back. And damn it all, she'd lost her husband barely a year ago.

She'd only just started to venture into the dating world and she hadn't slept with anyone. She couldn't deny, though, that she craved companionship. She'd missed these sorts of meals and conversations with a man, sharing daily life. And she didn't know how to reconcile that with her fear of investing in another relationship.

"Oh, there's no question that I've changed," he admitted. "But we're talking about you. I know you're funny and I see your smile, but it's so dark."

Playing with her spoon, stirring it through the stew, she shrugged to keep her eyes from lingering on his bold jaw. Yet dropping her gaze only brought into view his strong hand holding the mug of beer.

She cleared her throat. "It's called seeing the world." Of course she wasn't doe-eyed anymore. Reality had forced her to adapt her fairy-tale dreams.

"Not everyone lets the world make them into a cynic. I know you've been hurt, but—"

"But nothing. I don't think you're one to offer advice on getting over loss." Her head tilted toward the baby's room. Pushing out her chair, she stood, attentive and determined. "I think I heard Fleur again."

Thankfully.

* * *

He would have thought she was lying about the baby needing her. And perhaps that had been her original intent in shooting up from the table to get away from his attempt at a more serious conversation.

But now the baby's screams were piercing, so much so even Kota was running in circles, agitated and fretting.

They'd both dashed to Glenna's room, where the portable crib had been set up. Broderick's heart hammered at the distress—hell, ear-popping misery—in Fleur's cries. He scooped her from the crib, pulled her close, but the cries didn't stop.

Working as a team, wordlessly he and Glenna channeled through the obvious. They changed her diaper. Tried to feed her, but Fleur rejected the bottle and it wasn't really feeding time, anyway. They burped her again and again in case it was gas. They took her temperature. Played music. Kept quiet. Gave her a bath.

And now nothing worked except pacing the floor.

He held the baby to his shoulder and patted her back like he'd seen the child care workers do at the on-site center. But damn it all, it wasn't working. "I think I'm doing something wrong." His forehead creased, anxiety flooding back into him.

"You're doing fine." Glenna shook her head, offering an encouraging smile.

"Maybe I'm patting too hard." What if he was hurting her? He would never be able to live with himself if that was the case.

"You're probably not patting hard enough. She's not a butterfly."

Her lashes sure felt like butterflies against his cheek. Damp butterflies as big fat tears rolled down her face. God, she was breaking his heart and driving him batty at all once.

Glenna walked out of the room, motioning him to follow. "I'm no baby expert, not by a long shot, so let's see if we can figure this out. You keep holding her and I'll run an internet search. Somewhere on some forum there is an answer for this." She opened the laptop and began typing.

How had his parents survived this? Before the internet? Especially with so many kids, even a set of twins?

The thought of Breanna blindsided him.

He swallowed hard and yanked his thoughts back to the present. To this baby. This moment. And how he could get this kid calmed down and go outside to deal with the memory of losing his younger sister, Naomi's twin. "Have you found anything out on that internet search of yours? Because if you've run out of ideas, I'll look around for a while."

Glenna waved a hand at him dismissively as she scanned, a harried expression spreading across her face. Somehow...somehow this worried, harried look suited her. Glenna's dedication to this child, even in this moment of uncertainty, made her all the more alluring. She glanced up at him, exhaustion mixing with fire. "I'm still looking…"

"Look harder. Maybe we can take her on a plane

ride in lieu of a car ride." He knew his parents had used the car to put Breanna asleep. They joked that even as an infant, she'd needed to travel, to move. He shoved the painful thought back down, needing to focus on the present. On Fleur. On being there for his possible daughter.

"I'm not comfortable with an impromptu plane ride in the middle of the night with no flight plan."

Damn. That made sense. His unease grew as Fleur's crying continued, becoming even more urgent. For the first time in his life, Broderick felt the tug of failure, felt he wasn't enough for the task at hand. "Fair enough. Maybe you could walk her and I'll look on the internet."

"What else do you expect to find? We've covered all the steps in Baby Care 101."

"I have friends I can ask." There were a few people at the office dancing in his mind's eye. Surely one of them would know what to do.

"Are you planning to tell them what's going on in your life? Because I'm not sure that's wise."

"I can be subtle," he protested, heat flooding his cheeks.

She burst out laughing, launching a fresh wail from the baby.

Broderick winced, not sure when he could recall feeling this helpless. "Shh, shh, shh, Fleur. I'm here. I would sing, but my voice would hurt your ears."

Glenna leaned back in her chair, her eyes softening. "You really are doing everything right. Just keep walking and let her know you're there. When you're tired, I'll have a turn. We'll keep walking until she falls asleep. Maybe it doesn't sound like much of a plan, but from everything I've read, it's a timeless one."

"Timeless plan it is. I guess there is nothing left to do." He paced around the room, slowly and gently rocking Fleur.

"If someone had told me a year ago I'd be in a cabin with you and a baby, I would have called them a lunatic. And yet here we are." She folded her arms across her chest, her expression surprisingly light and inviting.

"Yes, this was never a scenario that entered my mind, either." He walked toward the window, drawn to the blanket of stars.

"Funny how things work."

He chuckled wryly. "Truth."

Silence hung between them for a moment.

Actual silence. The baby had stopped crying.

In a softer voice, one barely above a whisper, he asked, "What do we do now?"

She pointed at the crib. "All the blogs say you should lay the baby down while she's drowsy. Let's do that. I'll be right there with you for moral support."

On creeping toes, they made their way into the small nook area with the crib. Broderick laid the baby down carefully.

The only sounds were the quiet ones of a snoozing baby. His eyes met Glenna's. And though shadows cloaked her face, she seemed calm. A small smile rested on her lips.

He realized right then why he'd jumped at the idea of making their relationship more serious.

This wasn't a casual weekend rekindling for him.

Ten

The next morning, Glenna woke to streaks of sunlight coming in through the windows. The days were lengthening, but Alaska nights were still long, even in the spring. She stretched and wriggled her toes to work away the remnants of sleep.

And then the night came flooding back.

How she and Broderick had decided to stay in the room with Fleur. How they'd fallen asleep while waiting to make sure she was really okay. They'd had the small parenting victory of figuring it out together.

She found herself drawn to the word *together*.

Sleep had come so quickly in that domestic scene. She opened her eyes fast and found—

The bed was empty. The pillow held the indention of his head and the Egyptian cotton sheets were tangled. The fat comforter dragged off his side of the bed. She touched the space and found the fine thread count sheets to be cool. He'd been up for a while.

Her gaze skirted over to the portable crib. It was empty, as well, the whale-and-fish mobile swaying lightly. The house was silent, with not even a bark from Kota.

Curiosity, along with a hint of panic, wafted through her.

She swung her legs off the bed, the furry rug warm on her bare feet. She tiptoed along the floor until she found her fleece-lined slippers and shoved her chilly feet inside. Threading her fingers through her tangled mass of hair, she padded to the bedroom door...

And oh my, the sight took her breath away.

Broderick stood by the soaring window overlooking the water, Fleur in the crook of his arm as he fed her the last of a bottle. Kota snoozed on the sofa with an unrepentant air. The whole tableau had such a natural look, the epitome of so many dreams she'd had for her life back when she was married to Gage.

Except right now, she was having trouble remembering her dead husband's face. All she saw was Broderick's tender expression as he talked to the swaddled infant.

"Shh, little one. Let's not wake up Glenna. She's been taking such very good care of you. She needs her rest." He set aside the bottle and eased the baby to his shoulder, and a rag draped over his shirt. He patted her back a little awkwardly still, but was becoming better and better with practice. A tiny foot in a pink bootie slipped free from the blanket and Broderick ensured the little leg was well covered.

His attempt touched Glenna deeply. She leaned against the door frame, tilted her head to the side as Broderick continued, "You know, one day I'll help you with homework. We'll discuss $y=mx+b$ and other mathematical equations that will blow away the rest of the class. And I'm sure you will be the smartest kid in the room. Hey, probably even the whole school—"

Then he stopped short, as if feeling Glenna's gaze. He turned on his bare heels, a sheepish grin on his face. "She seems to like math."

Glenna laughed softly and padded closer, her heart warmer than her toes curling inside the fleece slippers. "So much so, you put her right to sleep."

He ducked his head to peer at Fleur's face. "Well, what do you know? She's out like a light." He softened his voice. "It's mind boggling how much babies sleep. Seems like she just woke up."

Glenna extended her arms, wanting a turn, hungry to feel that tiny weight curled against her. "Thank you for taking her so I could sleep in this morning."

"We're a team here. For the new family order."

Broderick placed Fleur in her arms, his hands brushing hers in the process. Little sparks of electricity danced in her stomach, awareness building.

Her gaze flashed up to his. Any question about whether or not he felt the same way was answered in that heated look. Her heartbeat quickened; her breath caught.

How long could she pretend that attraction didn't

affect her? From the look in his eyes, pretense was drawing to a close.

Glenna gingerly walked to the crib and set Fleur down, caught in a dream of what this life might be. After smiling down at the baby, she kissed the top of Fleur's head. The moment her lips touched skin, she realized those test results would be back soon. The business merger would begin. And this idyllic time away would end.

Sooner rather than later.

She didn't know if she wanted to accept Broderick's offer of a serious relationship. But she knew she wanted him. And she didn't have much time left here with him. This was her chance. She intended to take it. Well, as soon as she brushed her teeth. And wasn't that a silly thought?

She sprinted into the bathroom, afraid if she took too long the baby would wake up again. Was this what being a parent felt like?

As quickly as the thought tickled at her mind and tempted her bruised heart, she pushed it aside, before it could distract her. Hurt her.

She stepped out of the bathroom in winter silk pajamas, checked on the baby again and made her way back into the living room. Broderick stood facing the window, his shoulders as broad and strong as ever. Before she could second-guess herself, she walked across the thick woolen rug and slid her arms around his waist. Wrapping herself around him.

Only for a moment did the muscles along his back

ripple with tension, with awareness. Then he placed his hand over hers.

"Glenna, you have to know if we do this, it won't be a one-time deal."

His words unnerved her even as the reverberation of the sound of his voice rumbled over her skin where she lay her cheek against him.

Still, she also knew those words were very likely true. "I hear what you're saying."

She wanted him, and yes, more than once. Her body ached for a deep and sensual meeting and mating with this man. He felt so good against her, his muscled body, his callused fingers that were still so gentle.

"Good. I'm glad we have that cleared up." He turned and faced her, brushing her hair back with his hands as she linked her arms around his neck.

She trembled against him, her whole body attuned to his and the way they seemed to fit together so naturally. Her breasts tightened against the fabric of her silk winter sleepwear, the tips aching for his touch, for his mouth. It didn't help that his fingers teased a path down the back of her neck and along her half bared shoulder, making her skin tingle in anticipation.

Her head fell back to give him better access… and she caught sight of his cell phone and computer resting on an end table, bringing reminders of work too easily to mind. Damn it, she wanted to will them away. "I do have to wonder, though, Broderick. How are we going to work together if we start sleeping together? Everything is complicated enough—"

He pressed a finger to her mouth, his voice a soft brush of sound along her ear. "Let's talk after. We're in agreement now, aren't we?"

To hell with computers and phones and business. This was their pocket of time together.

She all but swayed on her feet from longing as she nipped the tip of his finger. "Yes, we are."

Arching up, she pressed her mouth to his, and oh my, he tasted familiar and new and exciting all at once. His tongue stroked over hers in a way that made her weak with longing. Hungry for more. She opened to him, pressing herself into him. The past blended with the present as she remembered that weekend so long ago and kisses they'd shared more recently. She'd always been attracted to him. Somehow, she knew that wouldn't change with time. She knew that wasn't the same as love, but damn, the feeling was strong.

Powerful.

Her hands took on a frenzied life and hunger of their own as she tore at his T-shirt, bunching the cotton in her fists and pulling it up over his head. And as she felt the air brush her stomach, she realized he'd done the same with her sleep shirt, until they both stood flesh to flesh. Only their pants and her sports bra separated them.

He was all muscles and calluses and hints of bristly masculine hair under her questing hands, his strength formidable as she took in the breadth of his shoulders. He felt so good she could just melt all over him. Into him. She dropped kisses onto his shoulder and down his powerful chest.

She played her fingers along the warm planes of his shoulder blades, down his spine as he backed her toward the fireplace. Their shoes fell away; his jeans and her sleep pants peeled down and off without either of them pulling away from the kiss. When she stumbled slightly the hard strength of his arms banded around her. Lowering her. Laying her to rest on the bearskin rug. The fur tickled her tingling skin, almost as tempting as Broderick's lips kissing up the inside of one leg and down the other.

Moving upward again, he tugged at her waistband of her panties with his teeth, teasing without pulling them off, then nuzzled her stomach, stroking until it seemed his touch and mouth were everywhere. When she thought she would combust from the fire inside her, he stretched over her and kissed her. Oh my, how she'd missed being kissed, and kissed well.

"More, now," she whispered, nipping his bottom lip. "We can go slower the next time."

"Next time," he growled softly. "I like the sound of that."

Cool air brushed over her tightening nipples an instant before his mouth closed over one taught peak. His tongue flicked and circled until she writhed with pleasure. He teased the other with the stroke of his nimble fingers, and she ached to feel him, too, and explore, relearn the texture of him. Her hand glided down to cradle the rigid length of him, to stroke.

To remember.

His breath hissed from between his teeth, an encouraging moan stoking her desire until it was hotter than the flames in the fireplace. "My jeans. Pass me my jeans, so I can protect you."

She didn't question him for a second, just used her other hand to reach off to the side and pat until she found his pants, the denim still warm from his body. She fished in the pocket until she found his wallet, the condom. More than one. But for now, one would do.

He kicked free of his boxers at the same time he twisted the string along the hip of her bikini panties. Her lacy underwear had long been a favorite indulgence to wear under all the layers of clothes she needed to stay warm. Although right now, staying warm was the last concern on her mind.

Between the fire and this fiery man, her body was a delicious lava pool of need. She tore open the condom packet and sheathed him, held him. His eyes met and held hers as she guided him…

Inside.

A moan of pleasure rolled up her throat and free. She arched against him, the sweet pressure of him filling her, that first deep thrust almost sending her over the edge. She could have chalked it up to abstinence, but she knew better. Their connection was chemistry on overload. There was no need analyzing. And quite frankly, the last thing she wanted to do now was think. She only wanted to feel and absorb every sensation.

The bristle along his legs was a sweet abrasion as she brought her own legs up to wrap around his waist. The taste of the perspiration as she kissed his jaw was like ambrosia. The slick glide of their bodies against each other ramped up her pleasure with every roll of her hips. Each gasp of pleasure took in the scent of him mixed with the earthy air of the fireplace.

Timeless aromas and feelings imprinted themselves in her mind as they made love in their cabin, sequestered away from the world.

The pressure and pleasure built inside her in time with his speeding heartbeat until she flew apart in his arms. The force of her orgasm sent her head pressing back into the bear rug. She held Broderick tighter, closer, taking every ripple of pleasure from the moment. And more. His shudder of completion sent a fresh wave through her, stronger than before.

So much. Almost too much. Making her wonder how she would ever be able to walk away from him a second time.

Not in a million years did Broderick imagine one day he would be sitting in sweats at his cabin retreat, sharing computer files back and forth with Glenna— who was currently rocking the hell out of her sleep pants and one of his T-shirts.

They had been crunching numbers for the past hour, preparing a plan for their parents to present to the board. Glenna sat with her knee tucked to her chest as she looked at the screen.

How in the world was he supposed to concentrate with this woman in the room?

After their frenzied lovemaking, he'd taken his time. They'd moved to his bed, where he'd touched and tasted every sweet inch of her luscious body.

They'd showered together, the steam of the water and their passion mingling to fog the oversize stall. A shared snack had rejuvenated them enough that he would never again be able to stand in that kitchen without thinking about lifting her onto the counter. Finally, they'd both fallen into an exhausted slumber, waking long enough only to feed the baby and go back to sleep.

Being with her shook him. Rattled him right down to the core. More than he'd expected. He had to figure this out. How to be with her in the middle of their crazy family drama.

He took a sip of coffee, counting on the caffeine to provide focus and answers. Breathing in the spiced smell of the hazelnut coffee—Glenna's favorite—he tried to focus on the low hum of the baby monitor. Still, remaining focused was hard.

He picked up an apple pastry from the plate and bit off a large bite, chewing thoughtfully.

"This financial merger is going to send us all through the ringer." Glenna's husky voice caressed him, spurring him to find the best fit for her in this new age of their merged companies.

He nodded, glancing at the various career positions on the screen. Glenna was organized and dynamic. Perhaps more of a public relations job would suit her?

"Also, about our parents… I'm still processing that." Glenna rubbed her temples before scooping up a puffed pastry. She tore an edge off, popped it in her mouth.

"I sure as hell never saw that coming between the

two of them," Broderick agreed, wondering about the implications of his father and Glenna's mother as a joined force in the business world.

"They kept their secret well. Maybe we can keep what we're doing a secret, too?" Glenna teased, looking at him sidelong.

A rumbling laugh rolled up his throat. "We didn't manage that before when our families never saw each other. I doubt we'll be able to pull it off now that we'll be working together." He dimmed the light on his screen, then swiveled to really look at her. "Not to mention sitting at the holiday dinner table together. At least our discovering them in the shower kept them from eloping. I would have been sad to miss out on the wedding."

"It's still…strange. Thinking of the two of them together."

He sipped his coffee, the java warming him. "Unexpected, that's for sure. But maybe it's a sign we should take a fresh look at what happened between us in the past. We've spent so many years avoiding each other. Hearing horror stories about the other family's sharkish dealings."

"I wonder how long they've felt this way?" Glenna's voice trailed off and she seemed miles away from him as she turned to stare out the window.

"Is that your way of ignoring my question?"

She snapped back into focus, eyes narrowing as she tugged a hair band off her wrist and gathered her tousled locks on top of her head. It seemed that pulling that mane back helped her create distance. "It's my way of staying on topic. Your question is another subject for another time. Back to our parents. How long do you think this has been going on?"

Broderick couldn't help but ask, "You think our parents cheated with each other?"

"No—at least I don't think so. Even considering it makes me…unsettled. But I wonder if they had feelings for each other. It's upsetting to think back on my childhood and wonder if it was a lie." She tore off another piece of the pastry and chewed thoughtfully.

He could tell the idea upset her, perhaps because of her own experiences.

"Do you think you're feeling this way because of your husband? Afraid to trust people could really love each other and be honest? I would apologize for asking such a personal question, but our lives are already tangled up—and they will be forever." He needed to know what was going on with her. Wanted to understand.

"It's okay. You're not saying anything I haven't already wondered, too. Life is just so…" She bit her lip and waved her hand in the air.

"Complicated," he offered, giving her fingers a reassuring squeeze. At the touch, he saw her eyes widen. Dropping her hand, he smiled at her encouragingly.

She grabbed her coffee mug, holding tight to the handle. "Definitely. I take it you don't think there were any feelings between them until recently."

"I think if there were, they didn't act on them. I know none of this changes who my mother was or how much she loved her kids." He could feel emotions pull at him—the pain of losing his mother and sister so palpable.

"That's beautiful."

"The stew was one of her recipes. She only taught me and Breanna how to make it. She said just the oldest children—son and daughter—got to have the recipe."

His throat tightened and his eyes grew heavy with feeling. The conversation wasn't supposed to go here. Broderick ran a hand through his hair, trying to regain his composure.

Fraying nerves made all the colors in the room too bright.

Glancing at his drained mug, he got up from his seat and headed to the coffeepot. He focused on the darkness of the drink, the way the aroma filled the air.

Broderick needed his defenses back up if he was going to make it through the remaining days with Glenna. But damn the next few days. He needed to figure out his next few words.

Reality pushed hard on him.

Glenna couldn't help but make the most of the chance to study Broderick as he walked across the cabin's living space to refill his coffee. With his back to her, he reached for the carafe, his shoulders heaving with a heavy sigh.

In that moment, she realized that she'd pushed on a wound in his personal life that hadn't healed, still caused so much pain. Part of her considered giving him space, but a larger part of her accepted that she needed to know more. With his proposition looming between them and the DNA test due any moment, she had decisions to make.

Despite telling him no, she couldn't help but consider his offer of starting something long-term with him, to join forces for Fleur and the company—and for that explosive attraction between them. What he said made sense. But still she balked, craving a sign.

Wanting to understand him better.

Needing to tend to this wound he'd been dealt.

She understood what it was like to be emotionally raw. And really understood the value of sharing the painful memories, of giving them breath and life. So difficult, but she would push a little bit more, a little more gently.

Glenna set aside her laptop and shoved back her chair to join him at the counter. She rested a tentative hand on his solid biceps. "I'm sorry if I pushed too much with the personal questions."

"No need to apologize. We've crossed a line here today and there's no going back to the way things were."

Oh Lord. The line. She'd known that at the time, but it didn't really sink in until this moment. In this space between syllables where she and Broderick were undefined.

Kota trotted up behind her, his white-and-black snout finding her fingertips. Scratching between his ears, Glenna waited for whatever Broderick would say next. For wherever this conversation was going.

In spite of having just downed an apple pastry, Broderick pulled out the leftover stew from the fridge without looking at her. He grabbed a bowl from the cabinet and a ladle from a drawer. Eyes flicking toward her, he pointed at the food. An offer.

She shook her head, anchored herself by stroking the fluffy fur on Kota's head. Broderick shrugged, still not speaking as he poured a few scoops into the bowl.

Maybe she should stop waiting for him to share and instead offer up something of her past. For the first time, it dawned on her how closed off she'd been, expecting everything to come from him. Afraid of being vulnerable.

Glenna poured another cup of coffee, added sweetener along with half and half. Absently stirring it, she realized what she had to do, what she needed to share, how to connect with him in hopes of coming to her decision. "We rigged a zip line through the backyard over a frozen pond."

He paused midbite. "You did…what?"

"A zip line. We were young engineers and ecologically minded kids. We figured out the aerodynamics." She held the mug with two hands, blew on it to cool it. Then took a sip and nodded at him.

His face relaxed, seemed less contorted than before. "I imagine that was quite a ride."

"We were kids. Our math was good." She set the mug down, laughing softly. "Our sewing? Not so good. The sling gave way."

"Ouch. Broken bones?" he asked, pulling the stew from the microwave.

"A fracture and a dunking." She shuddered at the memory.

"Through the ice?"

She nodded. "It was scary. So scary."

"You're the one who went through?"

"Worse. My cousin Sage did. But I knew it had to be my fault." She'd been the mastermind—the one who'd suggested the zip line. Sage had volunteered to go first, trying to prove she was brave. It had been a rite of passage, one that went terribly awry.

"How did you and your brothers haul her out?"

There had been no option except action. Even now, Glenna could feel her brothers' grip as she'd gone in after Sage. Her arms reaching and thrashing in the cold water for any trace of her cousin.

"We held on to each other and went in as a human chain until she was safe."

"You could have all died."

"She would have done the same for us. We were close. You understand. You have siblings."

"We were more...competitive. But yes, I like to think we would have gone to any extreme to save each other. Actually, I know we would have." He looked down at his stew.

Glenna ran a light, encouraging hand down his back. "What about you and your sister Breanna?"

"Ah, so now we get to the heart of what you're pushing for. You want the emotional grist."

She chose her words carefully. "Your sister is

clearly important to you and yet you and your family don't mention her very often."

"It was—is—painful to think about her," he admitted hoarsely, staring down into his bowl of stew. "Most people don't know, but we didn't get a clean goodbye. Long after that crash, we were tormented by calls from sick bastards who wanted to milk us for money with everything from offers to speak to her in the afterlife to people who said they'd seen her. None of those leads turned out, of course. My father had each one investigated, no matter how crazy."

"But I thought she died in the crash…"

"She did. Her body was—" he choked up "—badly burned. But there were a couple of teeth in the ashes. Her teeth. All evidence pointed to her dying that day and no ransom note ever came. We waited, even hoped for a long while, because at least that hell was better than death."

"I am so very sorry. I had no idea your family went through that. That had to be difficult for all of you, not having the official closure of saying goodbye to your sister and mother."

"Mom's body was thrown from the plane before the fire really took hold. She was already…gone. It was hell, but at least we knew."

Forget distance and boundaries. Glenna closed the space between them, slid her arms around his waist and rested her head against his chest. "Oh, Broderick, I am so sorry."

He set aside his stew and held her closer. "My father was always nervous about someone kidnapping us because of his fortune. After the crash, I thought he would lose his mind. He assigned a bodyguard to each of us twenty-four-seven. I can assure you, that gets awkward at school." He chuckled.

She didn't. Because her heart was breaking for him. She touched his face, stroking his cheek. He captured her arm to stop her, and slowly, deliberately, kissed the inside of her wrist.

"Glenna, the last thing I want is your pity. The very last thing."

His mouth sealed over hers with unmistakable possession.

Eleven

After the passionate night they'd shared, Broderick couldn't imagine they would have the energy to make love again. But already he felt desire building inside him with each stroke of his tongue against hers. His erection throbbed between them. No question, he was ready, eager, wanted to be inside her again.

Morning sunlight streamed through the skylights over them in the kitchen, helping guide him, giving him an even better view of temptation.

Glenna's arms glided up, her hands behind his neck, fingers feathering lightly. He knew the feel of her touch against his skin, the tips of her fingers teasing along his hairline. Yes, he remembered. And she was everything from all those years ago—and more.

His hands traced her sides, then cradled the sweet

curve of her bottom. He lifted her, bringing her flush against him until her feet dangled off the floor. Her personality was so strong and magnificent he sometimes forgot she was so much shorter than him, slighter in frame. She was an oxymoron of delicate power.

Her legs locked around his waist. He carried her to the kitchen table, kissing her every step of the way.

Carefully, he eased her back on the tabletop. A sexy smile spread across her face in invitation. Her hair fanned across the wood. She looked like a goddess—gorgeous, sexy, strong.

And his for the taking.

His hands stroked her shoulders, her breasts, the smooth flat planes of her stomach, until he swept her silk pajama pants down. Her sigh of anticipation drew a growl of appreciation from him.

Dropping to his knees between her legs, he caressed her, nuzzled, found her with his tongue. Her hands gripped him in encouragement. Each time they were together, he learned more about her body, her wants and her desires. He burned to glean more insights; pleasuring her damn well pleasured him.

With each touch and tease along the tight bundle of nerves, he called on the ways he knew to bring her to completion in an intense rush. Her breath came faster and faster until…

Yes.

Her back arched in pleasure as she bit back cry after cry. Her legs clamped harder at his shoulders, her fingers digging in. He guided her as each aftershock rippled through her, until she relaxed with a sated sigh.

He inched up her body and cradled her face in his hands. "Let's be together. Really together."

"You don't have to say that to get me in bed." Her eyes were heavy lidded, her cheeks still flushed from her release.

"I noticed. Now say you're ready to get serious with me." He cradled a breast in his hand, his thumb stroking over the tightening peak.

She clasped his wrist. "Don't use sex as leverage."

"Be with me." He rested his forehead against hers, his voice hoarse with emotion.

"I heard you the first time." Easing out from under him, she righted her clothes again. He could feel her body tense as she moved away.

"I'm going to keep asking." He couldn't back down from his proposition. Not now. Not after the last few nights together. Not after all their shared history and twined futures.

"Even if it turns out Fleur isn't your baby, you want me in your life long-term?" Her tone was dark, as sharp as a knife leveled at his heart.

Broderick crossed his arms, staring hard at her. "You think I want to be with you for free babysitting services? I can pay someone for that."

Child care wasn't his concern. He had enough money to make sure Fleur had the best care possible, around the clock.

Glenna's eyes turned melancholy—with a hint of

steel. "I think you're looking for a mother for her, and I'm the one who comes with the least complications."

She raked back her hair, a shudder falling from her lips down to her toes. Broderick couldn't help but note how ragged she sounded.

He laughed darkly. "If you actually believe you come without complications then you are not thinking clearly."

Nothing about their situation was simple. A decades-long family feud, engaged parents…a passion that had danced between them since they were teenagers. Now precious baby Fleur.

"There's no need to be sarcastic." She paced away from him. Creating distance. Old habits. Just like a decade ago.

She doubted him? Well, he could dissuade her of that notion. This time, he'd make sure she didn't walk away.

He followed her and rested his hands on her shoulders. "I'm serious."

"Then I will rephrase." Her face was sad, her hair a tousled mess. "You know I'm the person least likely to complicate your life by falling in love with you."

Ouch. "That's harsh. And also a weird compliment, if you think every woman is at risk of succumbing to my charms."

He ran a light finger down her arm. For a moment she leaned toward him. Almost an answer to his call.

Her face softened. "I don't mean to insinuate that your feelings don't matter. You're offering something serious. That's a big deal. But I know you're not in love with me."

Love. A word that only brought pain.

She had to know that. He'd thought his plan would appeal to her. God knows, the idea of a lifelong passionate friendship enticed him. A way to be connected to someone without the emotional risk, without laying bare his heart and having his scars flayed open.

Had he been wrong in his approach with Glenna? If so, it wouldn't be the first time he'd royally screwed things up when it came to this woman—or to relationships overall. "Is that what you want me to say?"

"No!" She almost shouted the word, then glanced toward the baby's room. "No," she said more softly. "I just want you to stop pressuring me. Give me time to think. I hear what you're saying and how it makes sense. But everything is happening so fast. I need time to sort through the implications. I need time. Please."

Spinning away before he could answer, she raced back to the baby's room, the room where Glenna slept, too. Without him.

Strange how he'd been on board with an analytical decision when it came to himself, but hearing that same need for logic come out of Glenna's mouth was hard to accept.

Eyes averted, she closed the door behind her, making it clear he was not welcome.

Glenna gave up trying to sleep by five in the morning. She'd been tossing and turning restlessly all night.

The silence in the cabin was deafening. Her fault. She'd kept to her room after her argument with Broderick, stepping out only to get supplies for Fleur. However, the time alone gave her too much room to think. And feel guilty for the way she'd rejected him out of hand.

With heavy, burning eyes, Glenna glanced at the baby. Fleur still slept, her little breaths providing a steady rhythm to the early morning.

Dragging heavy limbs from bed, Glenna wondered again what to think of all this. She made her way to the crib, drinking in the peaceful scene.

She had enough financial means to make it as a single mother if Fleur became her responsibility. But if Fleur was Broderick's… Sadness slid into her throat, forming a lump at the thought of losing daily contact with the child.

In such a short amount of time, she'd become bonded to the baby. She enjoyed Fleur. And sharing the baby's smiles and sweetness with Broderick.

Thinking back to Broderick's proposition had her stomach moving like an out-of-control Ferris wheel. Perhaps…perhaps they did make a pretty good team.

Was his suggestion of attempting a real relationship just ill timed?

On tiptoes, she walked out of the room with a rumbling stomach. In the still dark hours of the morning, she made her way toward the fridge.

The stress of the last few nights translated into a sweet tooth. Time for leftover tiramisu and a glass of milk.

She could hear it calling her name.

Lifting the container from the fridge, she caught movement out of the side of her eye. For a terrifying moment, Glenna convinced herself there was an intruder.

As her vision adjusted, she recognized the form. Broderick sprawled out on the sofa.

Relief washed through her.

"Oh my God, you scared me. I thought you'd gone to bed." Her free hand covering her mouth, she willed her heartbeat to return to normal.

He sat up, stretching, a blanket around his waist. "I fell asleep here."

The sexy timbre of his morning voice stirred something inside her, reminding her of things he'd whispered in her ear last night. The sweet litany of lover's words that made her feel beautiful. Desirable.

"I'm sorry to have woken you." Sheepishly looking at her plate of dessert, she raised it to him.

"Is the baby okay? I can feed her." All remnants of sleep left his face.

"She's sleeping well. I'm the one who was hungry." She held up a spoon. "Tiramisu for breakfast. Want some?"

"I'm good for now." He stoked the embers in the fireplace back into a blaze. "Thanks."

Broderick tossed two thinner logs into the grate. The dance of the flames reflected on his bare chest, turning the rippled muscles to burnished bronze.

Glenna sat on a bar stool, the leather cover creaking as she settled. She traced the wood grain along the breakfast bar, circling the food in front of her. "I owe you an apology for the way I behaved last night. And a thank-you for all you've done to help since we got here."

"No apologies or thanks necessary." His gaze fixed hard on the fire.

She tipped her head to the side. "Ah, come on. Your mother's stew recipe was epic."

Rising, he grinned. Half a grin, anyway. "Glad you enjoyed it."

"I liked hearing things about your family, too. Those stories make it easier for me to envision how the business is going to work after the merger. How we can all make it work." She hoped, anyway, because there wasn't a choice. The company merger was going to happen.

And a merger—a personal partnership—with Broderick?

She was still considering it.

"My dad had this annual tradition for the family. We all spent a winter weekend camping out in glass igloos. Sure, they were temperature controlled, but still it was the ultimate blending of sleeping outdoors under a clear sky with all the luxury of a hotel."

"That sounds amazing."

"It was. Dad did it for Mom, in recognition of her heritage, ours, too. You remember my mother was a quarter Inuit?" He shifted over on the sofa, making room for her.

His gesture inviting Glenna to sit with him touched her. Abandoning her breakfast, she slid from the stool and plopped down next to him. She tucked her feet by her side and positioned herself to face him. Even now, electricity hummed between them, adding fire to their conversation.

"That was incredibly thoughtful and romantic of him."

"I remember my parents being very in love. To be clear, she didn't grow up in an igloo." He chuckled. "She was the daughter of teachers, and was a teacher herself. She valued our education. My siblings and I joked we were homeschooled *and* went to public school." Pivoting on the couch, he faced her, the flickers of the fire enlivening his dark features.

"I remember when she died. The community was rocked by her death and your sister's. We all saw your father's grief." Glenna's lips formed a tight smile, and her heart was heavy with an acknowledgment of his suffering.

"You were at the funeral?" Silence fell for a moment, and even in the muted light, Glenna noted the lump is his throat. He swallowed hard, shaking his head. "I don't remember that day."

Her fingertips found his muscled arm. "We were there. My whole family."

"Thank you. I know your parents were considered a great romance, as well." He opened his hand and she slid her palm into his. Warmth and serenity seemed to emanate from him.

"I guess we both imagined our parents would stay single forever."

"The way you plan to stay single."

She avoided his searching gaze by looking toward the fire. "Work and family fill my life."

"Yet you are prepared to parent Fleur." He angled forward, examining their hands. He brought her knuckles to his lips, planted a soft kiss on them. Butterflies tickled her spine. He pressed on after a pause. "You have to realize that no matter whose child Fleur turns out to be, she's another symbol that our families need to unite."

"I want to raise her, regardless. You have to know that." She squeezed his hand before dropping it, coiling back into herself.

An exasperated sigh pushed out of his mouth with a hissing sound. "Then let me help you. You can be her mother no matter the outcome. We can parent her together."

He sounded so urgent. Yes, Glenna's past had made it difficult to trust, making it nearly impossible to believe his motives were pure. "Are you actually using that innocent baby to get me to give up my job with the company so you have a clear shot at CFO for the combined corporation?"

"No," he said, almost too emphatically. "Of course not. I'm just tossing options out there for us to discuss."

Ah, right. Options.

Which meant changes for her.

She shot up, headed back to the counter and the abandoned tiramisu. She shoveled a bite into her mouth, a poor substitute for all the things she hungered for in life right now. "Why don't you spell out these 'options' a little more clearly."

"You can consult, be the epitome of the working mom, have it all."

Ah, there it was. The catch. Disappointment filled her, over a hope she'd only just begun to embrace. "Why is this job so important to you?"

"Why is it important to you?" He matched her fiery tone with his own.

"It's my family's business. My legacy." Her work identity and her role in the family were integral to her self-concept, providing a rock to build on after her husband's cheating and then, later, his death. "There's your answer. Why should it be any different for a man than a woman?"

"How long have you been working for the company?"

"Are you going to dare say that because I'm a woman and was trying to start a family I care less somehow? Because if you go down that path…" Pacing restlessly, Glenna became mercury rising, fury mounting as her voice rose an octave.

He held up a hand, his eyes brokering for peace. "That's not what I meant."

"Are you sure? Because I'm not. If you find out you're Fleur's father, will you cut down your hours to work part-time?" She read his face, then her brows rose in bittersweet victory. "I thought not."

He began to speak, but stopped, his gaze pushing past her, above her. Growing…softer as he focused on the skylight. Following his glance, she found herself settled by the bit of northern lights visible. Blues, purples and pinks streaking across the sky in a shimmering nimbus. For a moment, the fight left the room. Or at least went on pause.

She nibbled her bottom lip. "I never get tired of seeing this."

"Me, either. My sister says this is why it's so important we're careful about the pipeline." Alaska's unearthly beauty never grew old for him.

"She's right. Our state, this place, is a treasure to protect. The Dakotas, too." Glenna couldn't keep the regret from her voice as she asked, "How can we have so much in common and be so far apart at the same time?"

"We don't have to be far apart." He said it quietly, without fuss or his usual hustling pressure. Genuine. Earnest.

Maybe he was right. Perhaps her own stubbornness wasn't that different from his. Without compromise they would never run the company or parent well. With so much at stake, she needed to take a step toward trust.

Her heart sped up ten beats faster than normal. *Leap.*

It wasn't her normal policy, but it felt right. Leaning back on the countertop, she felt the words in her heart before they came out of her mouth. "Okay," she answered before she could second-guess herself. "Let's be a real couple."

Broderick's face twisted in surprise. He blinked. Once. Twice. As if blinking replied to her words. She saw his disbelief fade, traded for happiness. And yes, she saw victory in his expression, too.

"Really? Wait, don't answer that. I don't want you changing your mind."

In a moment, he had closed the distance between them. Strong arms found her waist, lifted her up. They spun, her head back in a wicked laugh, hair fanning around her.

Broderick brought her back down. Kissed her deeply, his hand cradling the back of her neck.

Anticipation pulsated between them.

A sharp ping burst into the air.

Then another.

Broderick's ring tone.

He set her down, grabbed the phone off the counter. Moments that felt like hours passed as Glenna watched him take the call.

"Yes. Okay. I understand. We'll be there." An abrupt conversation. Everything about his features changed as he hung up.

"There's news. Good news and, um, I-don't-know news."

"What the hell does that mean?" she asked in frustration.

"Good news? The authorities have found Deborah and she's continuing to assert she wants to sign over her legal rights to the family of Fleur's father."

Relief and trepidation warred in Glenna's stomach. "And the other news?"

"The DNA test is back. Except the lab won't reveal the results to anyone except Fleur's family. They're asking us both to come in, but they won't say which of us they wish to speak to."

Just like that, Glenna knew this moment would change everything. They wouldn't have the opportunity to start a relationship on even footing, where neither of them knew who had parental rights to Fleur.

The scales were going to shift.

The next several hours blurred. She barely registered the too-bright light of the waiting room or how uncomfortable her green chair was.

They'd packed up everything and made it back to Anchorage in record time, with little conversation beyond the practical words needed to move things forward. For the past half hour, they'd been outside the doctor's office. Waiting.

Her stomach somersaulted, revolting against her.

Broderick paced with baby Fleur. Had it really only been a few days ago that holding her had seemed to scare him to bits? Now he looked as though they'd been together since birth. Fleur rested comfortably in his arms. While that should have reassured some part of Glenna, her heart hurt.

They'd both told their respective families they didn't need support here today. This was a matter they could handle alone. But Glenna's sister-in-law, Shana, saw through that line and made sure to be in the doctor's waiting room, anyway.

Glancing down the hallway, Glenna watched the doctor talk on his phone. Torture. The information was so close to being revealed. So close to changing their lives.

Putting her hands in her lap, Glenna took a deep breath, trying to focus on that simple action.

Shana stroked Glenna's back, reassuring as ever.

In these moments, the world seemed so clear. Hindsight being twenty-twenty and all. Why didn't she delay the results? Why didn't she ask for that?

She wasn't ready to know the truth. Not really. A lump pushed into her throat.

Except she knew why they had come straightaway. She and Broderick had both rushed here. Once those results were in, they'd needed to get back to Anchorage as quickly as possible, for Fleur's sake. They couldn't risk even the slightest delay that could cause a hiccup in custody. Even with Deborah Wilson's signed statement surrendering rights to the baby, so much could go haywire. Fleur had to be the number one priority.

Which meant Glenna should have accepted his offer to start something real between them sooner. Any relationship—if it was still going to happen—would come second to fighting for custody of Fleur.

It had been a long, quiet flight home.

Images of what could have been her future sucker punched Glenna.

Shana's low, honeyed voice cut into her thoughts. "Are you sure you're ready for this?"

Blinking, Glenna sat up straight. "Of course. I have to be."

It was a lie and the words tasted like ashes in her mouth.

"For the baby or for the business?" Shana scrunched her nose, looking at Glenna sidelong.

"Both, of course. They're tied together because it's all about the future of our family."

"I hear you." Shana shook her head, cutting to the quick of the matter. "But that's still not my question. Are *you* going to be okay if you have to let the baby go?" She never pulled punches with Glenna. Always said what was needed, even if her words were difficult to confront.

"I have to be."

"Even if Broderick is the baby's father?"

Another question Glenna couldn't answer. She wasn't even sure if her answer mattered or not. But however this turned out…it would be difficult. Painful as hell, actually. Because, oh God, she wanted this baby to be hers. And even as she thought that, fast on the heels of that possibility was the reminder that becoming Fleur's mother meant she would have to face what a sham her marriage had been. Face the fact that Gage had broken his promises after the tremendous effort it had taken to repair their marriage after his first infidelity.

Or had it been his first?

Glenna swallowed down bile.

"Thank you for your concern. But I can't worry about what I can't control." If the baby was Broderick's, then would she always wonder if he'd asked her to play house with him just so she could be a surrogate caregiver? An easy two-for-one option that would take care of his child and streamline matters at work?

As much as she wanted to pour out her fears to Shana, she couldn't bring herself to say the words out loud for fear she would fall apart.

"You keep talking about the practical concerns, but there's so much more going on here than that. I can see it in your eyes." Shana rested a hand on Glenna's arm and squeezed lightly. "Honey, I can't help but worry you're going to get hurt."

Glenna felt transparent. So she pushed back, injecting ink into the situation.

"My heart is closed up tight." Her fist clenched involuntarily.

"Ah, honey, take care of yourself." Her sister-in-law slid an arm around Glenna's shoulders and hugged her close for a moment. "You know I love you as much as any sister. No in-law part to it."

For a moment, all Glenna could do was nod before speaking. "I know, and I feel the same."

"Good, very good." Shana hugged her tight and said with a catch in her voice, "Call me if you need me."

"In a heartbeat." Glenna hugged back before easing away. She hesitated, something keeping her from ending the conversation, after all. "And you? How are things? Are you all right?"

"Fine. Just tired… And no," Shana said with a sad smile. "I'm not pregnant. Definitely not."

"I'm sorry." She knew they'd been trying for so

long and understood the heartache of infertility all
too well. There were no words to make it easier. There
was no "right" thing to say.

"Thank you for not telling me 'It will happen.'
I'm really tired of that." A forced smile pressed her
lips tight—

A receptionist in a bright pink dress walked out,
clipboard in hand. Pushing a piece of mahogany hair
behind her ear, the woman cleared her throat.

The name she was about to call would be Fleur's
parent.

The moment seemed to last forever, tension building like a terrible storm. Glenna's breath caught in
her throat as she waited.

"Glenna Mikkelson-Powers, the doctor will see
you now."

Her stomach lurched with the reality that Fleur
was her baby. Her dead husband's child.

Her hand trembled as she pressed it to her lips, as if
somehow that could hold back the reality. "Gage," she
said in a tortured whisper. "Gage is Fleur's father."

So many thoughts jumbled on top of each other—
especially the realization that Gage had cheated again
in spite of his vow. He'd betrayed her. Once more.

Eyes flicking to Broderick, she took in his features
and the pain there, as well. A wave seemed to knock
into him, pushing against him with force. Heartache
twisted his normally handsome features, made him
clench his jaw.

He'd been hoping Fleur was his.

In that instant, Glenna realized how much he cared

about the baby, enough to offer a relationship to a woman he didn't love. Even though he was hurting, she realized that now his need to have Glenna as the baby's mother was gone.

Her chance to have something real with Broderick had ended.

Because even if he still wanted to take that leap for himself or family unity, her dead husband was Fleur's father.

And Glenna's already fragile ability to trust had just taken a fatal hit.

Twelve

Jeannie sagged back against the hospital vending machine, cradling a cup of coffee. Needing the caffeine, the warmth. And knowing it wouldn't come close to heating the chill inside her while she waited for Glenna to finish her meeting with the doctors. Broderick had left, his face stormy.

How would this family ever heal now? She hadn't even told them about her breakup with Jack. So much had been going on with the baby. Plus, she and Jack needed to talk practically about the merger plans that had already started…

Such a tangle.

Her heart ached for all of them. Her daughter's husband had cheated. God, that was such a betrayal, and there was no recourse to fix things since he was dead. This situation would have been so much easier if Broderick had been the father.

But he wasn't. And they had to deal with that.

The child was a part of their family.

Her family.

But Jack's?

Broderick said he still loved the child, but she and Jack had split and life was such a mess. She'd thought her heart couldn't hurt this much again.

She was wrong.

Heavy footfalls pulled her from her thoughts, familiar steps, steady and sure. Jack's. Her eyes closed as she drew in the scent of him and waited for him to speak.

"Jeannie, we need to talk."

Biting her bottom lip, she glanced down the hall toward the doctor's office. "Glenna—"

Jack held out her coat. "Her siblings are waiting. I told them to call you the minute she's done. Let's walk, outside. Please. I may be a businessman, but my thoughts work better out in the open. In my Alaska."

As much as she wanted to challenge him for taking over, she also saw the heartbreak in his eyes. She dropped her coffee into the trash and slid her arms into her parka. "How did you know I was feeling restless and in need of a walk?"

"It was a guess," he said, as he led her toward the small courtyard, with a path and benches cleared of snow. "We share so much in common with how we embrace this home of ours. Am I wrong?"

"Of course you're not," she answered as the doors

closed behind them. A brisk wind churned flurries and she shivered.

"You don't have to make that sound like a bad thing." He looped an arm around her and pulled her to his side, warming her through and through. "I happen to think it's very good. I like who you are—a boardroom goddess and an earthy woman all at once."

"Things haven't changed for the better with the news today. If anything, they've gotten more complicated." She'd missed talking to him, working problems through. She valued his feedback, as she knew he valued hers.

Had she been wrong to break things off between them? Even now, it seemed impossible to pull away from the warmth of his touch. The comfort of his embrace. How had she walked away from him the first time?

"I suspect that will be the case more times than we can count. Yes, things are complicated for us. But there's only one way around those problems."

She glanced up at him, his wind-ruddied face so handsome her teeth hurt. "What way would that be?"

He stopped and clasped her shoulders. "Together."

Her heart swelled to hear those words and she knew she had to pull back before she caved.

"Jack—"

"Jeannie, hold on. Listen, please. I'm not dismissing your concerns. God knows, the thought of having one of my kids walk away forever scares the hell out of me." His exhalation was full of emotion, swirling between them in a white cloud. "I know they're as stubborn as their old man. But I also know they're the amazing people they are, in great part, because Mary and I didn't compromise our principles. I suspect the same was true with how you brought up your brood."

She nodded, unable to deny it. And also unable to deny how much sense he was making. Could she trust him to put her fears to rest?

"Then you know, my dear, if you love me even half as much as I love you, we have to stay the course." He brushed a snowflake from her nose, then stroked her cheek, his gloves scratchy, but his touch gentle. "I love you. I want to spend the rest of my life with you and I believe you feel the same. You love me so much you were willing to give me up because in some convoluted way you thought that would make me happier."

She blinked back tears. "I can't bear the thought of causing you hurt."

"Jeannie, love. Being with you makes me happy." His words rang with certainty. "The thought of my life without you by my side is unbearable."

"And you are sure?" She had to ask again. Or maybe she just wanted to hear it, the truth that made her heart sing and gave her such joy and hope.

"Absolutely."

"Okay then." She blinked back the tears, nodding, peace rushing through her for the first time since she'd walked away from that pool. "We're getting married."

"On schedule." His tone left no room for misunderstanding.

"Yes." She laughed at her stubborn man, but then

she was stubborn, too, just subtler about it. Luckily, they wanted the same thing. "On schedule. As soon as possible, I want to be your wife, wearing your ring and sharing our lives."

He sealed their promise with a kiss, one that mingled all the textures of their feelings for each other. Friendship. Passion. Constancy. And before she finished her thought, he eased his mouth away.

He rested his forehead against hers. "Our children will come around and we will help them through the tough times life brings. Like now. We just need to be here to listen, support them, help if the opening arises. Jeannie, they *will* come around," he repeated.

"I think so, too."

And in that beautiful truth, she realized that even though they hadn't borne children together, they would celebrate and enjoy grandchildren together. In fact, they'd already welcomed their first. A precious, innocent life that had helped bring them all together.

Their beautiful future stretched out before her, a future full of family and love.

Fleur wasn't his daughter.

Glenna was walking away again.

Considering flying back to the cabin to lick his wounds, Broderick leaned on the dock railing at the Steele family compound, his coat zipped up tight and his Stetson holding firm in spite of the wind whipping off the water. Chunky bits of ice floated in the private bay, leaving spiky shards in their wake, much like the emotions inside him.

Once the doctor had called Glenna, making it clear she was the one with legal rights to Fleur, Broderick hadn't been able to stand around idle with his world crashing down on him. He'd pushed back the roaring denial and passed the baby over to Shana.

Then he'd made a hasty as hell retreat out of there.

He should be relieved to resume his old life before things had gone haywire. Before his reunion with Glenna. Before a certain infant had wriggled her way into his heart. But he wasn't relieved. Somewhere along the way, he'd grown to enjoy—deeply—that pattern at the cabin.

What he'd found with Glenna and Fleur had become about more than settling family drama. He wanted Glenna and Fleur in his life. Because damn it all, he couldn't deny the truth. They were firmly lodged in his heart.

And he didn't have a clue what to do next. Because he'd heard the pain and betrayal in Glenna's voice when she'd said, "Gage is Fleur's father."

He'd seen just as clearly in her eyes that she was crushed over this new infidelity from her now deceased husband, even though she loved the baby. There was no way Glenna would have faith in a man after the way that bastard had abused her trust.

So Broderick had left, giving her the space she would need to process her grief, with the support of her sister-in-law.

He gripped the dock railing until splinters pushed through his gloves. Normally, a dose of the outside world was a remedy for him. But as the cold wind pushed against his face, he felt an answering coldness rise deep within his chest.

A sharp inhalation burst through his lungs. Breath
had become hard. He'd hated the look of utter betrayal
on Glenna's normally composed face. He couldn't
protect her from the truth any more than he could
make Fleur his biological daughter.

He tried to stabilize his world. Another gust of
wind pushed on his chest, threatening to take his Stetson on a journey toward the bobbing seaplane in the
nearby bay. Hands flying fast to his head, he pushed
the hat back down. Took another breath and then let it
go toward the tall, sturdy mountains in the distance.

Everything had changed in the span of one sentence. His shoulders sagged under the weight of it
all. He felt a hand touch his shoulder. He knew without turning.

Glenna.

Somehow, she'd already come to him, only a couple hours after he'd left the doctor's office. Her hand
slid away and she stepped beside him, leaning on the
railing. Her purple parka was zipped up tight, the
hood on her head. Hints of hair blew from the side.

His throat raw from the wind and emotion, he
asked, "Where's Fleur?"

She gestured toward the mansion on the hilltop.
"Your family is watching her, and Kota, too."

"Good, that's good." He nodded tightly. "Why are
you here?"

"I wanted to check on you. You left so quickly we
didn't have a chance to speak."

"What more is there to say? You can't tell me you aren't in full retreat mode. So why are you here?"

Was it his imagination or did she flinch, her eyes dimming.

"It's…difficult. I'm reeling. But that doesn't mean I don't care about you."

Care? A wimpy damn word. Of course, he hadn't offered her much better. "I'm relieved to know her father isn't a stranger. That's good news for Fleur's security."

Glenna rested a gloved hand over his. "Broderick, I'm sorry you're hurting over Fleur not being yours."

"How do you know I'm not relieved?" he asked with a tight bravado he was far from feeling.

"Because…" She angled sideways, her cheeks and the tip of her nose pink from the cold air. "I could see it in your face, then and now. You're attached to her."

The baby wasn't the only one who'd become important to him. Seeing Glenna now, remembering what they'd shared, hurt like hell. Because he knew it was over.

"Who wouldn't?" he admitted, thinking back to the way the baby giggled. To all the innocence and trust in her alert eyes. "You're an incredibly capable woman. I believe you have this covered. You can handle parenthood without me." Though his words were dull and hollow, he attempted to smile at her encouragingly.

One of her eyebrows shot to the sky. Then he saw her features school themselves into boardroom neutrality.

Her chin trembled, before it tipped with strength. "I'm overwhelmed at the reality of being her mother. I can't deny that. And I have to admit that I'm tempted to ask for all the help I can get."

She was actually still considering coparenting with him? "But you don't trust me. Your husband hurt you. He betrayed you again. It doesn't matter what I feel. If you can't trust me, then there's no way a relationship between us will work."

Her forehead furrowed. "Don't put this all on me. You're the one who had the practical, no-emotions proposition. And now that I've accepted, you're ready to run. Or fly away. I can see it." She gestured to the plane.

"You're suddenly a mind reader?" Well, she was in a way, but realizing she read him so well only made him even more frustrated.

"Broderick, I don't know what you want from me." Her voice sounded weary, defeated.

As much as he wanted to take her up on the offer of seeing what they could be to each other, to help in a future with Fleur, he realized now that if he couldn't have it all with Glenna, it wouldn't be enough. He didn't want just an affair or a partnership for the baby, or for her to move in with him. He wanted her love.

But she loved a man who'd betrayed her, who'd damaged her heart quite possibly beyond repair. Broderick knew what it was like to live with the pain of loss and how it could damn near cripple a person's emotions.

They'd both suffered enough.

"Glenna, we're just torturing each other, dragging things out. This conversation is leading nowhere good."

The world pushed too hard on Broderick today. Fulfilling Glenna's prophecy, he practically ran to the plane. Slamming the door behind him, he took to the skies. Didn't care where he was headed.

So long as it wasn't here.

Glenna's thinly constructed scaffolding of emotional coping mechanisms began to give way as she watched the seaplane fade from view.

Broderick had left her.

Left her.

The realization tore at her already frayed nerves, slowed her heartbeat. How could he leave her without a real explanation?

Already, today had been too much. Her world had tilted when the receptionist called her name. The truth of her late husband's infidelities had crashed into her.

Somehow, she'd foolishly held out a sliver of hope that when she walked out on the dock to talk to Broderick, things would be okay. She'd make peace with him, at least for the moment. Doing that had been hard as hell on the heels of realizing Gage's betrayal, but she'd tried. And Broderick had literally run away from her. God, it hurt.

Too much.

Her heart ached, and she felt the melancholy in her bones.

"Come fishing with me," a rusty masculine voice demanded.

Jack Steele?

She turned to find that, sure enough, Broderick's father stood a few steps away. She hadn't even heard him walk across the planks of the dock.

His request more than stunned her. She spun on her heel. Jack stood in a heavy flannel shirt with two fishing poles. She blinked, taking him in, fighting back the tears that threatened to spill over. "Excuse me, sir? You want me to do what?"

"Girls can go fishing, too. My daughter learned early and I expect you to bait your own hook." He extended a sleek blue fishing rod in her direction.

"I'm not arguing. I'm just surprised that this is how you would choose to, um, bond." She chewed the inside of her lip and cast a nervous glance toward where the seaplane had been only a few minutes ago.

"That goes to show you don't know me or my family. I hope we can change that, for your sake and for my son's." He thrust the fishing pole at her along with a tackle box. "Let's walk farther down the shore, where my son hasn't scared away all the good fish with his takeoff. Give a little here, okay? Let's get to know each other."

Their boots clinked in time as they walked side by side on the dock. The midday sun sparkled along the cresting ripples of the water.

She laughed drily, attempting to go with the flow in this bizarre outing. "With all due respect, sir, it's not like we have a choice. You're marrying my mother, so we're going to see each other."

They made their way off the main dock, turning a corner. Their boots crunched on stray snow as they made their way out onto a fishing platform.

Glenna grabbed the bait bucket, then stuck her hand in the chilled water, searching for the right fish. Satisfied with the one she came up with, she back-hooked and cast her rod. They both heard the sound of the reel releasing the line far out into the bay.

Jack whistled softly. "Color me surprised. You're really good at that."

"My father taught me. In the early days of the business, all the extra cash went back into the company. We fished and hunted to save money on groceries. We ate well. Didn't Mom tell you?" Glenna spun the reel, comforted by the clicking sound.

"Hmm, not in so many words," he said. "Looks like we'll all be eating well. You'll be stocking the freezer." He cast his own line.

"This is better fresh. These days when I fish, we split it up among the staff."

Scanning the horizon, he said, "That's thoughtful."

"Our family is so large now, I may need to stay out here longer." Her breath caught for an instant over the word *family* connected to the Steeles and Mikkelsons. Her gaze drifted off to the empty horizon where Broderick had flown away. "Our family. I'm still getting used to the sound of that."

"Both of our families have been through a lot of pain, a lot of loss." Jack's dark eyes searched her face.

Glenna swallowed a lump in her throat. All she could do was nod.

His rod bent, went taut, then slack. Something had nibbled and gotten away. "I just have one more question."

"What would that be?" Glenna asked, reeling her line in. She sent it back out, and it landed with a resounding plop. Minor in comparison to the splash of a whale tail in the distance.

Broderick was out there somewhere on the horizon, hurting, aching from another loss. She couldn't help but worry about him and what he was feeling.

And she couldn't deny she still wanted him. She wanted to comfort him. Wasn't that why she'd come out on the dock in the first place, instead of rushing back to her own family home?

Heaven help her, she didn't want to let Broderick go.

Jack angled his head her way, mustache curving with his smile. "Why do you keep calling me sir?"

His question surprised her. "I'm, uh, just trying to keep from calling you Mr. Steele or, um, boss man?"

"At least you're not calling me that hard-nosed something or other, or worse." He pulled his line back in. Then gave another cast.

They laughed. The family feud seemed so distant, for this moment at least. "I'm just not sure what to call you."

"I prefer Jack, but that's up to you." His rod bowed deeply, and he fought with the line for a moment. Soon, he'd reeled in a fat, wriggling trout. "But we'll all have time, because there's no dodging each other. We are family. And family is everything."

Broderick was her family.

That fact truly dawned on her, causing her to re-evaluate the last few hours. He was family in the most important way. He'd never turned his back on her. She'd been the one pushing him away, even as far back as college. In spite of the pain of his losses, he'd still been willing to risk it all to commit to her.

He was a man of honor. A man of deep feelings. She knew that in her heart. Her mind had just been too stubborn to listen.

But not any longer. She turned to Jack. "Is there anyone here with a pilot's license who can fly me to Broderick?"

The cabin had been colonized with so much meaning over the last week.

Sure, he had memories of the cabin from childhood. However, the memories that attacked him now were of Glenna and baby Fleur.

He sat on the deck, trying to shove the past week out of his mind. But the hot tub undid any and all progress he'd made.

He looked skyward at the sound of an airplane engine, realizing what approached wasn't a seaplane, but a twin propeller plane with wheels.

The plane touched down beautifully on the lawn, settling in a surprisingly small area. Which meant it could be piloted only by his brother Marshall. He was one hell of an aviator, though these days Delaney was giving him a run for his money.

Marshall hopped out of the plane, with no hat, his curly hair in serious need of a cut as the wind tore at him. Family support. That had been something Broderick could always count on. He drew in a breath, ready to shout. Then he saw strawberry-blond hair and a slender frame. His breath caught as Glenna darted down the steps of the plane, clutching a simple overnight bag.

A feeling like hope kicked around in his gut. No. More than that.

A rush of love so strong it threatened to take him down faster than an Arctic wave.

Marshall stopped at the bottom of the deck and cupped his hands around his mouth to shout, "Brother, are you good with me leaving?"

Looking down the steps at Glenna, Broderick saw the hope glimmering in her blue eyes. He should never have walked away from her. Should have stayed and worked things out back on the Steele family dock. But maybe he was getting a second chance. A way to put the past behind them.

He shifted his attention back to his brother and nodded. "We're good, Marshall. Thank you."

Broderick walked down the steps as Glenna walked up. He reached for her overnight bag and resisted the urge to touch her. To haul her into his arms and hold her until they both froze to the spot.

They needed to talk. He wouldn't rush her. She was here, for him. Right now, that was everything.

Walking toward the cabin steps, he asked, "Where's Fleur? And Kota?"

"We have a family full of very qualified baby-sitters and puppy sitters who lined up to help."

"Fair enough." They walked into the house. A fire crackled in the hearth, casting an orange glow into the room. She shimmied out of her thick coat. Damn. Glenna was elegant even in dark wash jeans and a tan cashmere sweater. It didn't matter what she wore. She always took his breath away. He couldn't imagine ever seeing her and not wanting her.

Gesturing to the leather sofa, he asked the question searing his brain. "What are you doing here?"

She eyed him warily, half reaching for him, then pulling her hand back. "I came for you. For us. If you still want to talk." She sat on the sofa, cross-legged. "Really talk. You ran off before we even had a chance to let the news about Fleur settle in." She looked at her hands. "Before I had a chance to process what Gage had done."

God, that had to have hurt her. Broderick took her hand in his. "I'm sorry. Genuinely sorry. I know you loved him."

Her eyes met his, no tears. Just full of regret. "I'm finally learning to accept the marriage for what it was. Flawed, and likely destined to fail." Her mouth half tipped in a bittersweet smile. "You may have noticed, I don't deal well with failure."

Dealing with failure? That's something he understood well. Yet, he'd never shared the greatest failure of his life, and it wasn't a story that would come out easily.

However, Glenna had made the effort to chase him. It had gotten his attention. It had given him another chance at this relationship they seemed to be starting, and he needed to deserve it. He offered up a piece of his soul—an aspect of himself that he guarded carefully.

In a quiet voice, he began, "I'd like to share a story with you that will help you understand me better, a story passed down through my family."

Glenna stroked his hand softly, then curled her fingers around his. "I would like to hear it."

Hard as it was to say, he found he wanted to tell her. Very much. "My mom used to arrange sleigh rides for us."

"That's a beautiful memory." She stroked her thumb along the inside of his wrist.

He looked around the room, taking in the decor. He felt as if he saw the past, his former life, and the life that didn't have a chance to happen because of the plane crash. "She loved this place, her home state. We vacationed in the Dakotas when Dad had business, but this was home. For her. For us."

"She's the one you got the stew recipe from?"

"Her, and she got it from my grandmother. Yes. My mother wanted to teach us about how her Inuit grandparents lived as much as possible. We hunted, moose mostly, and fished, to fill freezers for orphanages and local food pantries. We still do."

"I've gotten a sampling of your father's fishing skills."

What? Interesting, and worth talking about later. Right now, he needed to stay on task. "Caribou, too, obviously. We even hunted some seals."

Surprise washed over her face. "You caught a seal?"

"With some serious help from my great-grandpa. I was more of a lightweight participant. It was a memorable day, to say the least. But I learned lessons from them that stay with me now."

"Such as?" she pressed.

He adjusted his body on the couch, facing her, hoping she would grasp the importance of what he was trying to explain. "In the pure Inuit culture, there was no social structure or class, no ownership. The earth and its resources belonged to all of us. It was shared property for living and hunting."

"Everyone was equal?"

"To a degree. There were people with a higher status based on things like seamstress skills. Being a shaman. Others. But you had to pull your weight." He chuckled. "Now that's a credo my father wrapped his brain around."

A small smile played at the corners of her lips. For the first time since she'd arrived at the cabin today, she seemed calmer. More assured. "I can see more and more how our parents are going to mesh well."

"My grandparents made sure we heard the legends directly from them, not from a book. Like the legend of the Qalupalik. She was green and slimy and lived in the water. She hummed and would draw bad children to the waves. If you wandered away from your parents, she would slip you in a pouch on her back and take you to her watery home to live with her other kids. You would never see your family again."

The story had terrified him and his siblings when they were younger. A small memory wafted through his mind as he recalled how Delaney had cried the first time she'd heard it.

"Sounds like a certain fish movie that's quite popular."

He spread his hands. "Hey, when a life lesson works, it works." Which brought him to his point, what he needed her to know. "We also had our own werewolf legend about the Adlet. They were said to have the lower body of a wolf and the upper body of a human—"

"Like centaurs," Glenna said, leaning forward. Her attention fully on him.

Good. This was progress.

"I guess so. And apparently, they still roam. My brothers and I tried to hunt one once. We had to turn back because Naomi tagged along and Aiden followed her... Are you just being polite? You have to have heard all of this."

"I haven't heard it this way. Not from you." She narrowed her eyes as if trying to discern his intent. "What are you trying to tell me?"

The thoughts sliced at his insides like more shards of ice. "Naomi and Brea were twins. They were supposed to have that special bond. People worried more about her after we lost Brea, and I understand that. But she and I were close, too." A pained smile tugged at his mouth. "She was even given the name I was supposed to have if I'd been a girl. She was my baby sister. I was supposed to protect her."

He swallowed hard before continuing, "Since my sister Brea died, I've felt like half a person—like the legend of Adlet. I didn't think I had anything of substance to offer another person, not until these past days with you and Fleur."

Glenna's blue eyes melted, tears glimmering. She squeezed his hand. "For a confident businessman, you vastly underestimate yourself."

Hope kicked up another level, along with awareness from the feel of her hand in his. "I think you just complimented me."

"I did. You are an incredible man on so many levels." She took his other hand, as well, pinning him with an intense gaze. "Why would you want to settle for a loveless relationship? I accepted a half measure in my marriage for years and I can tell you, it eats at your very soul."

He ached for her and the pain she'd been through. She deserved better.

He wanted to give her better. "I wasn't settling, not by a longshot. You are everything I could ever want in my life. I realize now I was more concerned about being what you need in *your* life."

Her eyes filled with more of those tears and she moved forward as he leaned toward her. Their mouths met, not in a kiss of unbridled passion, but one of relief, connection.

And love.

He felt the emotion without hearing the word. The connection went beyond the electrical current that set their senses on fire. This feeling was more like northern lights of the soul.

Her hands rested against his chest, sending his heart slugging against his ribs. "Broderick," she whispered against his lips, "we haven't made our report to the board. What about our jobs?"

"I'll step aside," he said without hesitation. And he meant it.

To win over Glenna, there was no sacrifice too great. And with her at his side, he knew he could achieve success beyond any preconceived plans he'd set for his life. She opened his horizons.

Enriched his life.

Her eyebrows shot up in shock. "You'll do that? You can't possibly mean to give up your job, your stake in the Steele business."

"No job is more important than you." He meant those words more than any he'd ever spoken. "There is more to life than work. There is family."

"But...your job *is* your family."

"No. Not anymore," he said simply.

"You really mean this." Amazement entered her blue eyes as she scanned his face.

"Whatever I need to do to prove to you I want to be the man you deserve."

She flattened a hand to his chest. "You don't have to do this for me."

He smiled unrepentantly. "It's not like I'm lacking financially. I work because I want to, not because I need to. I can consult. Spend more time with you. With Fleur."

She blinked fast, nibbling her lower lip, then blurted out, "What if we both consult?"

"Run that by me again? I'm not sure I heard right. You've been so adamant about your family legacy. I don't expect some kind of quid pro quo on the job-quitting front. We'll both be making sacrifices along the way. I get that. And I also get that our relationship, our marriage, will be worth it."

"Broderick…" She squeezed his hand hard. "*Family.* Isn't that what we're talking about? You and I building a family together? Marriage, even. This is *our* legacy, one we build together. We can consult for the company and create our own schedules."

He stroked her face, feeling a joy he was beginning to realize could be his for life. "I like the sound of what you're saying, but I want to make sure you really understand you don't have to give up your career for me."

"Oh, Broderick, don't you see? I'm not giving up anything. I'm healing broken relationships and facing new challenges instead of just protecting myself from possible hurts. I'm embracing a life with you. And if our parents say no to this plan of ours—" she inhaled deeply "—then *we*, you and I—a family— become oh, say, accountants maybe, and live off our portfolios and hunt and catch fish while we play with Kota and bring up Fleur. Our daughter."

The beauty of her offer and the magnitude of her sacrifice filled him, making him feel whole for the first time in a very long while. "I am totally in love with your plan, and I'm totally in love with you, Glenna."

Her arms slid around his neck and she wriggled closer, leaning into him. The softness of her body against his fit with perfection, giving off a hint of the scent of almonds. "Well, isn't that a magnificent co-incidence? Because I am wildly, passionately in love with you, too, Broderick Steele."

And if he had any remaining doubts—which he didn't—he intended to prove just how strong their love was. He hauled her closer and gently rolled her to the bearskin rug where he would prove it all night long, for a lifetime.

Epilogue

Two weeks later

Glenna knew she wasn't the only mother ever to spend time simply gazing at her baby, so she refused to feel guilty about her lazy afternoon in the sprawling Steele family home, watching Fleur sleep in her swing. Nearby, Naomi worked on her tablet, her dark head bent over the screen as she tapped and scrolled. The quiet hum of the swing motor and the soft taps were the only sounds in the sunroom, and Glenna's life felt absolutely perfect as she watched the baby's head cuddle deeper into the side of the pink cushioning.

Glenna's whole world had changed since the "bachelorette" party for Jeannie in this room, the day

Fleur had come into their lives. Now, she felt at home with the Steele family, her heart expanding to take in all of Broderick's relations. Turning from Fleur's swing, Glenna peered out one tall window where a slight snow fell outside. Below, Broderick sat easily on his horse, returning from a ride with his family.

Her heart flipped in her chest. Broderick was such a strong man of honor. The love of her life. She still could hardly believe how much joy filled her world these days.

A breathy baby sigh drew her attention back to the room. Fleur's eyes were fluttering awake as she cooed happily, but Naomi's brow was deeply furrowed as she stared at her tablet.

Glenna leaned toward Naomi. "Are you alright?"

Broderick's sister looked up, her face smoothing. "Yes, just preoccupied." She set aside her tablet, and reached into the baby swing to scoop up Fleur. "Come here to Aunt Naomi."

"You're a natural with her."

Naomi shook a fuzzy bear rattle in front of the infant's face. "I love babies."

Glenna hesitated to mention children further. She understood too well how sensitive fertility issues could be. Broderick had told her about Naomi's cancer battle as a teen, and how Naomi's eggs had been frozen for a possible in vitro fertilization procedure later. What a traumatic thing for a teen to have to think about. "Well, Fleur definitely adores Aunt Naomi."

Naomi leaned her forehead to the baby's, then gave

Fleur the gentlest nose to nose kiss. "I know people see me as a work hard, party hard type, but family is important to me. Much of my workaholic nature comes from wanting to pull my weight."

"You're invaluable to the company." Glenna had never seen anything to give her the impression that Naomi was a wild child, but she'd heard the rumors. Sometimes, she knew, those labels could be unfairly earned.

Naomi's dogged determination made her an indomitable attorney. They were lucky to have her on their side. Still, there was a flicker of insecurity on the woman's face that surprised Glenna.

"I'll feel better once I've figured out a way to land Royce Miller's research for our company."

Royce Miller? That was a lofty goal. The recluse's oil industry inventions that melded efficiency with environmental safety were legendary—and much sought after by their competitors. "It would be a coup to land him—or even get a peek at his research. Of course, gaining access to even speak with him would be a good start."

Behind them, the exterior door opened a moment before footsteps sounded on the tile. Fleur heard it too, her little face straining to turn toward the noise before Naomi shuffled sideways.

A moment later, Broderick stood in the doorway in his jacket and Stetson, a dusting of snow on his shoulders. His eyes locked on Glenna right away, an electric look passing between them before he swept off his Stetson. Her skin heated, anticipation curling her toes at just the sight of the man she loved. How was it possible he made her so breathless with just a simple look?

Naomi cleared her throat, standing with the baby in her arms. "Glenna, how about I take the little one and feed her a bottle. It'll be good practice for…uh… one day. I imagine you two new parents could use some time alone."

"Are you sure you don't mind?" Glenna asked without taking her eyes off Broderick's.

Laughing softly, Naomi angled past. "I don't mind at all." She elbowed her brother on the way out. "Have fun."

Glenna walked to Broderick and slipped her arms around his neck, breathing in his scent. "Did you have a good ride?"

"I sure did." He skimmed a kiss along her mouth. "Although it would have been better with you along."

His touch gave her butterflies.

"For a gruff businessman, you sure have turned into a romantic."

"You bring out the best in me." He swept his hand along her hair. "And I mean that."

"Thank you. I do believe we were meant for each other."

His smile made her senses tingle. He backed away, his fingers trailing down her arm. "I think it's time we made this very official."

She angled her head. "What do you mean?"

He dropped to one knee and pulled a ring box from his jacket pocket. "Glenna, I was going to take you out for a romantic meal, tonight—and I still want to do that. But when I looked into your eyes just now, I couldn't wait any longer."

Emotion swelled. Her hopes and happiness were all tied up in this man and their future together.

She pressed her hand to her heart, savoring every detail of the moment to keep it in her memory so she could relive it again and again. "The feeling is mutual."

She wanted every day to be like this one, spent with Fleur and Broderick, surrounded by family.

A smile creased his sun-ruddied face. "Glenna, my love, my lover, my life, will you do me the great honor of becoming my wife?"

Her heart squeezed around the words. She dropped to her knees in front of him, clasping her hands around his holding the ring box. "Of course I will. I'm yours and I'm so glad you're mine. Forever."

He opened the ring box to reveal…a stunning canary yellow, square cut diamond. He slid it on her finger and she realized her fingers were trembling just a little. The ring was a perfect fit. Just like their love.

"Oh my," she whispered, extending her hand and capturing the sunlight in the facets. Rainbows floated around the room from the bright, beautiful stone. "It's gorgeous. How did you know it was the perfect choice?"

He kissed her nose. "I had some help from your mother and your sister. So, I take that to mean you like it?"

She liked what it symbolized more than anything. But the ring was breathtaking.

"I do," she said, thinking how someday she would say those two words to him again. She couldn't wait to speak their vows for all the world to hear. "And I have an idea. Let's skip dinner out and celebrate in our suite."

His eyes went a shade darker as he sent her a heated look that smoldered over her skin.

Clasping her hand, he stood, guiding her with him. "I think that's a brilliant idea, from my brilliant future wife."

* * * * *

Get 2 Free Books,
Plus 2 Free Gifts—
just for trying the Reader Service!

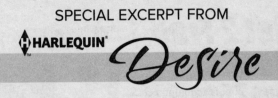
"You'll get to meet my brother tonight."

Penelope was embarrassed she didn't know a thing about
another Ferguson sibling. She'd only been in Texas for a
year, and between juggling her new business, moving into
her apartment and handling crises for the Dallas elite, she
hadn't climbed the Ferguson family tree any higher than
Chase and Stefanie.

"Perfect timing," Chase said, his eyes going over her
shoulder to welcome a new arrival.

"Hey, hey, big brother."

Now, that...that was a drawl.

The back of her neck prickled. She recognized the voice
instantly. It sent warmth pooling in her belly and lower. It
stood her nipples on end. The Texas accent over her shoulder
was a tad thicker than Chase's, but not as lazy as it'd been

two weeks ago. Not like it was when she'd invited him home and he'd leaned close, his lips brushing the shell of her ear.

Lead the way, gorgeous.

Squaring her shoulders, Pen prayed Zach had the shortest memory ever, and turned to make his acquaintance.

Correction: reacquaintance.

She was floored by broad shoulders outlined by a sharp black tux, longish dark blond hair smoothed away from his handsome face and the greenest eyes she'd ever seen. Zach had been gorgeous the first time she'd laid eyes on him, but his current look suited the air of control and power swirling around him.

A primal, hidden part of her wanted to lean into his solid form and rest in his capable, strong arms again. As tempting as reaching out to him was, she wouldn't. She'd had her night with him. She was in the process of assembling a firm bedrock for her fragile, rebuilt business and she refused to let her world fall apart because of a sexy man with a dimple.

A dimple that was notably missing since he was gaping at her with shock. His poker face needed work.

"I'll be damned," Zach muttered. "I didn't expect to see you here."

"That makes two of us," Pen said, and then she polished off half her champagne in one long drink.

Don't miss
LONE STAR LOVERS
by Jessica Lemmon, the first book in the
DALLAS BILLIONAIRES CLUB *trilogy!*

Available March 2018 wherever
Harlequin® Desire books and ebooks are sold.

www.Harlequin.com

LOVE
Harlequin
romance?

Join our Harlequin community to share your thoughts and connect with other romance readers!

Be the first to find out about promotions, news, and exclusive content!

Sign up for the Harlequin e-newsletter and download a free book from any series at

www.TryHarlequin.com

CONNECT WITH US AT:

Harlequin.com/Community

Facebook.com/HarlequinBooks

Twitter.com/HarlequinBooks

Instagram.com/HarlequinBooks

Pinterest.com/HarlequinBooks

ReaderService.com

**ROMANCE WHEN
YOU NEED IT**

HSOCIAL2017

Reward the book lover in you!

Earn points from all your Harlequin book purchases from wherever you shop.

Turn your points into *FREE BOOKS* of your choice
OR
EXCLUSIVE GIFTS from your favorite authors or series.

Join for FREE today at
www.HarlequinMyRewards.com.

Harlequin My Rewards is a free program (no fees) without any commitments or obligations.

MYR17